FINALLY

Doms of Destiny, Colorado 10

Chloe Lang

MENAGE EVERLASTING

Siren Publishing, Inc.
www.SirenPublishing.com

A SIREN PUBLISHING BOOK
IMPRINT: Ménage Everlasting

FINALLY FOUND
Copyright © 2015 by Chloe Lang

ISBN: 978-1-63259-088-6

First Printing: March 2015

Cover design by Les Byerley
All art and logo copyright © 2015 by Siren Publishing, Inc.

Printed in the U.S.A.

PUBLISHER
Siren Publishing, Inc.
www.SirenPublishing.com

DEDICATION

To my sweet sister, Lisa. You are always there for me no matter what I'm going through. Love you.

FINALLY FOUND

Doms of Destiny, Colorado 10

CHLOE LANG
Copyright © 2015

Chapter One

Carrie Doss glanced at the emergency exit just three feet from the table where she sat. Always having an escape plan in mind was something *he* had taught her a very long time ago.

But it wasn't just out of habit her current focus was on the door, which she'd noted her first day on the job at the diner. The exit had been quite easy to spot with the words "Alarm will sound when opened" across the big metal panic bar. No matter what shift she worked—early morning, breakfast, lunch, dinner, or late night—Carrie kept that door in view, in case *he* came through the front entrance.

She hadn't seen the con artist reverend in thirteen years, but the very thought of him made her blood turn icy and her insides storm. Could the female customer sitting across from her be on the bastard's payroll? Even if not, the woman had way too much information. The well-dressed lady had come into the diner and ordered pie and coffee. Not unusual. The eatery was one of the premier places in Dallas to get award winning, delicious desserts. Having a killer sweet tooth, Carrie had applied to be a waitress at The Little Spot Diner the very day she'd entered the city limits. That was only sixty days ago. Normally she would have at least another month before she packed her bags for another city, another place where she could remain anonymous.

Bags? She only had one, the big red suitcase that was never far from her and was always locked. Right now, it was inside the trunk of her car, a 2005 red Chevy Malibu, which was parked on the side street by the diner.

The woman had introduced herself as "Jena." She was Carrie's last customer for tonight's shift. "You were once Carrie Clemens, correct?"

"No," she lied. "I've never gone by Carrie Clemens."

Jena had asked Carrie to sit and join her for dessert.

It had been so long since Carrie had any connection with another human being. Pie and coffee had sounded good to her, being more than a little hungry. Against better judgment, she'd agreed and took the seat opposite Jena. Now she knew it had been a mistake.

"I see." Jena glanced back at the laptop that she'd brought out after Carrie had sat down. The woman didn't look dangerous. Actually, Jena was quite attractive. Her emerald-green eyes were vibrant and her demeanor was warm.

Carrie took another bite of her apple pie, noting that Jena had pushed her half-eaten cherry pie to the side.

Jena might not appear a threat to most, but Carrie had also learned that looks could be deceiving. Rev. William Mayfield, or Brother Willie, as he'd preferred to be called, had always seemed harmless but definitely wasn't. Not only was he a con man, but he was also extremely abusive. She had many scars to prove it—both physically and mentally.

Looking up from her laptop, Jena fixed her stare on her. "You changed your name to Doss, right?"

"No. I've always been Carrie Doss," she lied as her apprehension continued to grow. *Who is this woman and what does she want with me?* The more questions Jena asked her the more she worried that there was a connection of some sort between Jena and the reverend. "I've never been a Clemens."

"Clemens" was the first name Willie had given her after the fire. *His name. One of many.* She'd learned later that his real last name was Mayfield. Brother Willie had never told her. Did he even remember it himself? Of course he did. Unlike her mind, the bastard's had no gaps, no missing weeks, months, or years.

She didn't remember the fire, only the smoke. That was a recurring nightmare that had never gone away. How many times over the years had the dark dream pushed her to consciousness and she awoke screaming? Until her fifth birthday, too many to number. She'd learned to stifle her screams to avoid Willie's rage. But even now, twenty-six years later and away from his wrath, she still suffered with the nightmarish memory. Until she turned five, Willie had held her tight any time the terrors came, telling her that everything would be okay. But on the night of her fifth birthday, when the smoke had seemed so real, his tenderness vanished. In its place, a dark cruelty erupted that she had to endure from then on while in his custody.

"Shut up, you little brat." He slapped her across the face.

She started wailing and he hit her again.

"Shut up. Shut up. Shut up." He covered her mouth with his big hand, shocking her into silence. "I have a sermon to deliver tomorrow."

He released her. She looked up at him, sniffling.

His lips twisted into that horrific smile she detested. "Disturb me again and you will feel my full wrath. You're mine now. Your parents are dead. They didn't want you. I did. I have a special plan for you, Carrie. You're too young to understand it now, but soon all will be revealed. But I will not tolerate any more of your stupid dreams. Do you understand me?"

With an all-consuming fear and tears streaming down from her eyes, she nodded.

Rev. Willie had been the one who told her about her parents' joint suicide. He'd rescued her from the blaze. Part of her still felt obligated to Willie despite all the horror she'd endured living with him.

She'd only been three at the time of her parents' deaths. *Three years old.* Her life before was only flashes of memories. She couldn't bring up the faces of her parents, though she could recall her mother's long auburn hair and her father's big booming voice.

"What about Armstrong? Did anyone ever call you by that name?" Jena's locks were similar to Carrie's mother's.

At least the way I remember them.

"No." Another lie. They came easily after so many years of being on the run.

The woman looked up from her laptop's screen. "What about 'Dixon?'"

"Never." Which was the truth. "I've never heard of that name before."

Jena seemed more disappointed in that answer than any of the others. "Did you ever live in Atlanta, Carrie?"

Atlanta. Los Angeles. Chicago. New York. Choosing to reside in the large cities of the US made it easier to go unnoticed and hopefully undetectable by Brother Willie.

"No, Jena. I never lived in Atlanta." She was done with being interrogated and pushed her chair back from the table. "My shift is over and I have to be back at the diner early in the morning." *But I will never come back here. Time to run again.*

The chance of Jena working for Willie didn't seem likely, but that didn't matter. The big question that haunted her was why had Jena tracked her down? Carrie knew most of the possible answers and none of them were in her favor. "I've enjoyed talking with you. Consider the pie and coffee on the house. I hope you come back again and we can talk more."

"Please, Carrie. Don't go. I know your brother."

Her heart skipped a beat. "My brother is dead. I have no family."

"No. He isn't. He survived the fire. Matt is my husband."

She did remember having a brother. Willie had always denied it whenever she brought it up, calling her delusional. Could Jena be telling the truth? Carrie had no memory of her brother other than his eyes, which only appeared in happy dreams.

"Wasn't your brother's name Matt, Carrie?"

"I honestly don't know." *The truth. This is dangerous.* She glanced at the exit. "I really have to be going."

Before she could bolt to the door, Jena pulled out a photo and pushed it across the table.

She looked down at the picture and froze in place. The hazel eyes of the man in the photo kept her from moving. *Those are the exact eyes I remember. In my dreams.*

"This is Matt. He's your brother. You thought he was dead. He also thought you were dead. Thank God, you were both wrong. I've been searching for you for months, Carrie. You recognize him, don't you?"

"He looks familiar, especially his eyes. But this can't be my brother, Jena." How was it possible, being only three when she'd last seen her sibling, she could remember the color and shape of his eyes? Could what Jena was saying to her really be true? Could her brother really have survived the fire, the smoke? Did she really have family still alive?

If he was alive, what impact had their parents' suicide had on him? Did he have nightmares like her? "Does this man in the photo remember having parents?"

"Yes." Smiling, Jena reached across the table to grab her hands. Instinctively, Carrie jerked back but kept her eyes locked in on the photo on the table.

"Jena, I don't know what to think of this." The truth. Again. The back of her neck tingled, a sign it was far past time to make an exit.

"I'm sure it is a great shock, but believe me, you are not alone anymore."

Not alone? That didn't seem possible. Not for her. Not after everything that had happened.

Stiffening, she asked Jena, "What does Matt want? Why did he send you and not come himself?"

"Long before I met Matt, he held on to the hope that you might have escaped the fire. But after years of searching for you himself, he finally gave up. I love him, Carrie. He's such a wonderful man. That's why I picked up where he left off. I didn't want to break his heart if I couldn't find you. But somewhere deep inside me I knew you were alive."

"How can you know I'm the Carrie you are looking for?"

"The resemblance alone is unbelievable. Do you realize that you and Matt have identical eyes, hair color, even your smiles are the same?"

Gazing back at the photo, she did recognize the similarities between her and Matt. Could she trust Jena? Could this man really be her brother? She had nothing to lose, but was that her real concern?

"If Matt is my brother, Jena, the best thing to happen would be for him to stay as far away from me as possible. It would be completely selfish of me to just drop into his life. You're his wife. You're a family."

"We are, Carrie. And you are part of that family."

Clinging to false hope was something she couldn't afford despite how much she wanted to. Survival, that was all she could focus on. "I have too much baggage, too much darkness. I can't meet him. It wouldn't be right. And I still think you're wrong." She shook her head and pushed the photo back across the table to Jena. "I'm not Matt's sister."

"But you are, Carrie." Jena held up the picture. *Those eyes. What if they are my brother's?* "I have no doubt about that." Jena's voice lowered and sadness washed over her face. "I have my own dark past.

I'm not sure what you are running from, Carrie, but I know you are on the run. I've been there myself. Aren't you tired of running? Please just let me help you."

Something that hadn't happened in a very long time shocked Carrie. She felt tears welling in her eyes. "Jena, I really want to believe you, but you don't understand. No one does."

"Then help me understand. No matter what has happened to you or whom you are afraid of, I will help you. Matt will help you, too." Jena handed her the photo once again, reinforcing her point. "You don't have to face your demons alone any longer."

She stared down at the face. A thought broke the surface of her consciousness. She was in a swing, her tiny three-year old legs dangling. Her brother pushed her.

"Higher, Matt. Please."

The memory faded. Her hands trembled. She had so few memories. This was a new one. No. It was an old one that had been trapped inside her mind. But now it was out. Free. Something she could recall again and again. *My brother's name is Matt.* The photo must've triggered the memory.

"How did you find me?"

"I knew what rocks to look under. I'm skilled in cyber detection. You've left a digital trail that I was able to follow." Jena sighed. "Carrie, I know you are Matt's sister. But I can tell you're still uneasy with me. If I were in your shoes, I would be uneasy, too. There's one foolproof way to find out. We could do a DNA test."

"A DNA test? I've heard that could take days or even weeks to get the results." *I can't stay long. In fact, I need to leave as soon as possible.* She'd already decided on her next stop two weeks earlier—Philadelphia.

"I have some connections that will speed the results. We can have them by tomorrow. Don't you want to know for certain if Matt is or isn't your brother?"

"Of course I want to know, but I'm so afraid."

What if the DNA test proved the Matt in the photo was her brother? What then? Go to meet him? But what would he think of her if he knew everything that had happened since the fire? And what if Jena's Matt was not her brother? Then she'd be back in the same situation. No, not the same. An even worse situation feeling more lost than ever.

Jena once again reached across the table for her hands, but this time she didn't pull back, longing for everything Jena believed to be true. "Carrie, trust me. Give me just one day. That's all I'm asking."

Against her better judgment, she said, "I'll do the DNA test. I really need to know the truth."

* * * *

Sitting on the edge of the bed next to Jena in the hotel room, Carrie watched her open the envelope with the test results.

No turning back now.

She'd thought about hitting the road for Philadelphia last night after leaving the diner, but she'd promised to follow Jena to her hotel, and a promise was a promise. Even after saying good-night to Jena and heading to her apartment, she'd considered not returning. Better to pack and get on the highway, never to look back. Why open up Pandora's box on her past? What good could come of it? Were there reasons her mind had locked away her memories for so long? Reasons that were darker than she could imagine?

But she couldn't leave. Not now. Jena had given her Matt's photo. She'd stared at it all night, getting only a couple of hours of sleep.

I'm not a coward. I'm going to face this no matter what.

She felt her heart beating fast in her chest. "I still don't know how you were able to get DNA results back so fast."

Jena smiled. "I have access to resources that are quite extensive. Now breathe, Carrie. You're holding your breath. I am certain what the papers will tell us. You are Matt's sister. So relax."

"Easier said than done. You're as nervous about this as I am." Carrie already liked Jena. She could even imagine them being friends if her world was more normal. But her world was never normal. "Your hands are shaking."

"It's only all the coffee I drank."

Carrie grinned. "Just coffee? Hardly."

Jena laughed. "Fine. Let's both take a couple of deep breaths to calm down."

Jena inhaled deeply, and she followed her example. It did seem to settle her nervousness a little.

"Here we go, Carrie." Jena glanced down at the papers in her hand.

Holding her breath once again, Carrie's anticipation shook her from head to toe. "So? What does it say?"

Before answering, Jena wrapped her arms around her.

Was the news good or bad? She wasn't sure. Jena seemed to be the type of person who would give a hug in celebration or to comfort. Which was it?

The answer came from Jena, whose eyes were filled with tears. "I finally found you. Nice to meet you, sister-in-law."

"It's true? Matt is my brother?"

"Yes."

Oh my God. "What now?"

"Now, I take you back to Colorado with me."

Feeling herself tense up a little, she said, "Jena, I'm not so sure that's a good idea. Shouldn't you tell Matt about me first?"

"It's a wonderful idea. Besides, I want to surprise him. How hard would it be to get a few days off for you?"

"Not hard at all." She laughed, unable to hold back her excitement. "I was planning on quitting today anyway." Speaking the truth felt so good.

"That makes me happy. What do you think about me canceling my flight and us taking the road trip together? I can buy the gas. Plus it will give us a chance to get to know one another more. There is so much I want to tell you."

"About Matt?"

"About Matt and Sean, my daughter Kimmie, and my mom. I want to tell you about everyone in our wonderful town, which is quite unusual for most people but the best place to live in the world in my opinion."

"Who's Sean?"

"We have the whole drive to talk, Carrie." Jena smiled. "Destiny, Colorado, changed my life. I have no doubt it will change yours, too."

Chapter Two

Josh Phong stood beside Matt Dixon's new horse, instructing Matt on how to put on the saddle, while his cousin Jacob did the same with Sean MacCabe. Both Appaloosas were exceptional examples of the breed. Matt and Sean's wife's horse, a beautiful paint mare, was already saddled and ready to go for the surprise. Another new horse and one pony were in stalls. All of them were gifts for the men's family members.

"You need to always stand on the horse's left side, place the saddle pad on its back, on the withers."

Holding the pad, Matt turned to him. "What are the withers, Josh?"

Josh and Jacob laughed.

"I still can't believe you are both from Texas and don't know a thing about horses," Jacob said with a smile.

"We actually drive cars in Dallas, Jacob." Sean grinned. "But I do own a pair of cowboy boots, if that helps." He lifted a pant leg, revealing one of them.

"I know you have a lot of work to do teaching us, guys," Matt said. "But we really want to do this."

"For Jena and for Kimmie," Sean added.

Josh could see how happy these two men were. They had a beautiful wife, a precious daughter, and a wonderful mother-in-law. They were the perfect Destiny family and everyone loved them. "We're happy to do it for a piece of Janet's delicious apple cake."

Jacob shrugged. "That's great if we can keep Gary from eating it all before you come over."

"Gary and Jena's mom have been dating for how long?" Jacob had run into Gary many times. He was Doc and Mitch Ryder's uncle.

"Quite a while," Matt said. "I bet he gives Janet a ring before the end of the year."

Buzz. Buzz.

Matt pulled out the device that all the members of Shannon's Elite carried, something they called an ROC, a blend of a cell and a tablet—but so much more.

"It's Easton Black, Sean." Matt spoke into the device. "Hey, boss. Yes. Uh-huh." Matt sighed. "We're out at Stone Ranch with Josh and Jacob. Sean and I can be at TBK in fifteen minutes." Matt put his ROC away.

"What's so urgent?" Sean asked, also a member of the local CIA cyberterrorism team.

"Cindy Trollinger has been spotted in Denver. Black has called everyone in."

Josh's gut tightened. Trollinger was Destiny's number-one enemy. Like her dead brother Kip, she was determined to destroy the town. She blamed its citizens for her brother's death and wanted revenge.

"Jena is supposed to be here within the hour," Sean said, pulling out his ROC. "Our surprise is ruined. Can't reach her, Matt. I'll try her cell."

"She's driving. I'm sure she has her ROC and cell turned off. You know how she is about safety," Matt said, turning his attention from Sean to him and Jacob. "Guys, I hate to leave you, but—"

"Go." Josh placed his hand on Matt's shoulder. Matt and Sean were good men and had done so much for Destiny. He admired them, glad to have their friendship. "We'll take the horses out and get them exercised. You have work to do."

"She's not answering her cell either," Sean said.

Matt handed Josh the saddle pad. "If Jena shows up here, please tell her to come straight to TBK. I'm sure Black will want to use some of her special skills in tracking down Trollinger's exact location."

Without another word, Matt and Sean ran to their truck.

"I hope they catch Trollinger before she hurts anyone else," Jacob said.

"We all do." He remembered all the havoc and heartache the deranged woman had caused. One of Shannon's Elite had lost their life because of Trollinger.

As Matt and Sean drove away, Jacob asked, "Should we keep Jena's horse saddled up? They all could use some exercise."

"Good idea." Josh was glad they were working these horses. It helped keep him from worrying about what Trollinger might be up to. "We can let the other horse and pony out in the pasture. We'll exercise them when we get back."

"Get back from where?"

"We can ride over to Lover's Beach and switch off from horse to horse. See how they do in town with traffic."

His cousin laughed. "Traffic? In Destiny? You've got to be kidding."

He smiled, remembering Jacob had grown up in St. Louis and Los Angeles, but spent his summers here in Destiny. Jacob's childhood had been filled with pain, so much so that he'd changed his last name. Now they were both Phongs, even though Josh's mom was Jacob's blood relation, not his dad.

"Maybe Destiny doesn't have a rush hour, but any horse in this county has to learn how to act in town. I'm sure that Matt, Sean, and Jena will ride them to the Wok for lunch once in a while."

"I bet you're right. Most of the ranching families do." Jacob cinched up the straps of the saddle on Sean's Appaloosa.

They walked the horses out of the barn just as a ten-year-old red Chevy drove up. Jena popped out of the passenger side, and a beauty with long, dark hair got out of the driver's side.

"Josh, who is that gorgeous woman with Jena?"

"I don't know, but I'm going to find out right now."

"Hi, guys." Jena walked up with the newcomer right behind her. "Where are Matt and Sean? They sent me a text to meet them here."

"They just left, Jena," he told her. "I'm surprised you didn't pass them."

"Carrie and I came up County 66."

Her name is Carrie. "Jena, Easton Black called. Cindy Trollinger has been spotted in Denver. Matt and Sean wanted us to tell you to head straight to TBK."

Carrie stepped up and petted Matt's horse. Her face was filled with appreciation.

"You've been around horses before?"

She smiled. "I have. Yes. I just love horses."

Josh felt his heart jump out of his chest. "Then you must have a nice seat."

Carrie frowned. "A what?"

"I–I mean a nice seat in the saddle. You know. You can ride, right?"

Jacob laughed. "Forgive him. He doesn't know how to act around someone as beautiful as you."

"And you do?" he shot back at his cousin, trying not to act like a fool.

Jacob grinned. "At the moment, better than you."

Jena turned to Carrie. "I wasn't expecting this. My surprise is ruined."

"That's exactly what Sean said a few minutes ago." He knew how perfect Jena was for Sean and for Matt.

Jena's eyebrows shot up. "Why would he say that? I didn't tell anyone I was bringing Carrie to Destiny."

He looked over at Jacob, hoping he would help him out of this mess, but his cousin just shrugged. "I don't want to spill the beans."

"Josh Phong, don't pull that with me." Jena's tone was sharp. "What's this about?"

"They have a surprise for you, but I don't want to ruin it."

Jacob smiled, turning his attention back to Jena's friend. "Nice to meet you, Carrie. I'm Jacob and this is my cousin, Josh."

"Carrie, I hate to do this, but I have to go. I'll drop you off at my house and get back with you as soon as possible. My mom can get you settled in."

"Sure. That's fine." Carrie continued petting the horses.

"Carrie, why don't you stay with us?" he said, more in control of himself than a moment ago. "Jacob and I were about to go on a ride."

"All three are saddled up. Two riders and three horses?" Her eyebrows rose. "It's like you were expecting someone else to arrive. Were you?"

Not wanting to give any clues to Jena about her surprise, he said, "Joe just called and said he can't be here. So we need another rider."

"Joe?" Jena looked perplexed.

"Oh, you know Joe. He lives in Clover." Trying to dodge another bullet, he turned back to Carrie, holding out the reins for her to Matt's horse. "What do you say?"

Her eyes lit up and she nodded. "Yes. I would love to go on a ride. Jena, the keys are in the ignition."

"Thanks." Jena gave her a hug and then got in the car.

When Jena drove off, Carrie jumped up in the saddle like she'd been doing it her whole life.

Maybe she had.

"Where to, fellas?"

Chapter Three

The Colorado sky was a bright blue. Not a single cloud could be seen. A few peaks still had snow, though most didn't since it was early August.

"What do you think of Colorado?" Riding beside the gorgeous woman, Jacob couldn't stop stealing quick glances at Carrie.

"This is the most beautiful place I've ever seen in my life."

Josh rode on the other side of her, also staring. "Even though I've lived here since I was born, I still am in awe at all the things I get to enjoy each and every day—majestic mountains, tall trees, rushing waterfalls, clear lakes, and all kinds of wildlife. It's all here."

Carrie smiled. "A little piece of heaven on earth. I'm surprised we can ride three horses side by side down this road. What if a car comes up on us?"

"Listen to her, Josh." Jacob laughed. "She's worried about Destiny traffic just like you were earlier. Don't worry, Carrie. If by some chance someone does come up on us, they're used to people traveling by horseback. They'll slow down and we can move to the side to let them pass."

"He's right," Josh said. "No one is in too big of a hurry here. We take our time to enjoy the scenery."

"I don't know about that, cousin. Remember when Jaris got his sight back? He drove that pickup down Main at nearly thirty miles per hour."

"Thirty miles an hour is speeding in Destiny?" Carrie grinned.

They told her the story about how Jaris's sight had suddenly returned.

"Jaris and Chance are lucky to have Kaylyn as their wife," Josh said.

He couldn't agree more. "Those three are so happy together."

"You two seem to know everything about everyone in Destiny."

"Not just us," Josh said. "In our town, everyone has each other's back. We're one big family."

"Sounds like privacy might be difficult here." Carrie's demeanor darkened.

Jacob sensed she had secrets—like he once had—and didn't want them getting out. "No worries, Carrie. Everyone respects one another in Destiny. I used to live in St. Louis, and I didn't even know my neighbor's name. It was all different for me when I moved here."

"Why did you come to Destiny to live, Jacob?"

Hearing her say his name thrilled him. "Josh's parents are my aunt and uncle. Since I was a kid I spent my summers here with them. I fell in love with Destiny."

She smiled. "Looking around, I can see why. What's that mountain called?" She pointed to the biggest one.

"That's Blue Arrow Peak," Josh told her. "There's some trails that you can take on horseback that will get you all the way to the edge of the snow cap."

"Really?"

"Yep. I've gone up the trail many times, and it is a beautiful ride. At the top, you come out on a place that lets you see for miles and miles. A great place for a picnic."

Josh, who was normally a smooth operator with women with at least a dozen or more pickup lines, was being so open and honest with Carrie. It was nice to see.

Jacob knew exactly why his cousin was reacting to Carrie the way he was. She was so charming and warm, though he continued to sense thick, tall walls guarding whatever troubled her so deeply.

"Listen to us, Jacob. We're doing all the talking. We should let Carrie tell us something about herself."

"There's not much to tell. How about we race to that bridge up ahead?" She didn't wait for them to answer, but kicked her horse into full speed.

Josh looked surprised. "What just happened? Did I say something wrong?"

"Carrie is hiding something and if you start prying, she'll shut down. I know. I used to be like her. Remember?"

"I'll never forget what you went through." Josh sighed. "We better catch up with her. She's way ahead."

When they reached Carrie, she was sitting in the saddle by the bridge's sign. "Looks like I won." She laughed. "What took you so long?"

"You cheated," he said, relishing how happy she seemed in this moment. Whatever pain she carried, she controlled it well.

"What's the story on the name of this bridge? Silver Spoon Bridge is very unusual."

Before Josh could give the real reason for the bridge's name, he said, "It was named after Mr. Spoon, who wore silver cufflinks every day."

She giggled. "I know you're pulling my leg, Jacob."

"Me? I would never do that."

"Trust me, I always know when someone is telling the truth or not. I have a keen knack for that."

"So do I, Carrie." It was a trait that he'd developed after suffering so much. In his heart he knew she'd dealt with her own trials, though he wasn't sure what it was.

"I'll tell you the real story," Josh said. "One of our most influential and beloved families in Destiny is the O'Learys. They are billionaires and many years ago donated a big portion of the proceeds to build the original bridge. This is actually the second one. The first one was blown up by a woman named Trollinger, but that's another story for another time. Anyway, the O'Learys thought the name would let anyone coming to Destiny know how lucky they were. Like getting their own silver spoon in their mouths. Hence the name."

"That's a better story, and I can tell it is the truth. See, Jacob?" Carrie teasingly shook her finger at him, like she was a teacher scolding a schoolboy. "Fibbing doesn't do anyone any good."

He sent her a wink. "I promise never to lie to you again. Now about the silver spoon Josh mentioned. Why don't we cross the bridge and you discover the Destiny we love? I don't know how you two feel, but I'm starving. I think lunch at my aunt and uncle's restaurant is next on the agenda."

"I'm hungry, too. That sounds—" Suddenly Carrie frowned. "Silver Spoon. Billionaires. Oh my God."

"What's wrong?"

"My suitcase is in the trunk of my car." Carrie closed her eyes tight and gripped the reins firmly. When she opened her eyes, he could see the panic behind the façade of calm. "It has everything I own in it."

Even though he remembered having little himself for years, something in her tone told him there was more to her worry about the suitcase than just her belongings.

"I'm sure it's fine," he told her, hoping to reassure her. "They have security at TBK."

"Please. Guys, can we skip lunch and go straight to my car?"

"Whatever you need, Carrie," Josh said.

"Absolutely." He could see how anxious she was in her face. "But you gave the keys to Jena, and she will be in a secured area that none of us will be able to access. We don't have the clearances."

She sighed. "I didn't realize it was that secure."

"Didn't you know that Jena is a member of a CIA team?"

"We talked about so many things on the way up to Destiny, but that never came up." Carrie smiled again, which put him at ease. "It does explain how she found me."

Jacob thought about trying to delve into more about that story, but decided against it. Instead he said, "So is lunch back on? You have to try Uncle Hiro's sesame chicken. It is out of this world."

She nodded. "Lead the way, cowboys."

* * * *

Willie got into the rental car, a nondescript white Nissan Versa. Cindy Trollinger had made all the arrangements for this trip. He didn't trust the bitch, but she had done something he hadn't been able to do.

Trollinger had found Carrie.

Wait until I get my hands on that cunt. After all I did for her, how could she have betrayed me?

He pulled onto Interstate 70. Only four hours to Money, the town close to Destiny. The little motel Trollinger had booked a couple of nights for him was called the Nickel and Dime Inn. Appropriate, since that's what he'd had to live on since Carrie had run away and stolen everything. *Bitch! You will pay.*

The call from Trollinger couldn't have come at a better time. One of the deacons at the church in Arkansas where he'd been filling in at the pulpit had uncovered one of his earlier identities. Now there was no hope of convincing the tiny congregation of elderly assholes to let him become their pastor.

Trollinger had made it clear what she wanted from him on the phone, but before she could commit fully demanded to meet in person.

Trollinger's office was impressive, though he knew it wasn't permanent. There were no personal photos, no awards on the shelves, nothing intimate that a space would normally have if lived in for any length of time at all. Likely only rented for the week just for the meeting with him. He appreciated her style and flair. Good-looking, too.

But he was much smarter than she gave him credit for.

Walking into Trollinger's building in Denver, he'd been greeted by two men who clearly were packing heat. The young man behind the counter, much less intimidating and wearing glasses, led him to her office.

Trollinger had met him with a warm smile. She stood and walked up to him, her gorgeous brown eyes locked on his. Her short dark hair was spiked. She wore a leather red mini, a lacy white top, and stilettos that accentuated her long legs. She turned to her assistant. "Thank you, Michael. That will be all."

The man left quickly without a word. It was obvious that this woman demanded absolute obedience from her underlings. *An iron fist. Nice.*

"Please have a seat, Reverend. I think you'll be thrilled by what my agency has turned up for you. We found the woman you've been looking for."

She'd already mentioned knowing about Carrie on their earlier phone call. "And?"

"Before I tell you, I have to get assurance you will do what we've agreed to."

"I swear it." He sent her his most winning smile, a smile that had landed him many followers and lots of money. Not to mention lots of women to fuck.

Trollinger didn't appear susceptible to any of his charms. On the phone call she intimated she knew about the fire in Mississippi. She might have the upper hand with him now, but he would make sure to get some dirt on her to even the playing field.

"Trust me, Reverend, we are going to do great work together. Carrie's location was just discovered by Jena, the wife of her brother."

Her brother? Fuck. "Where is the bitch?"

"I expect she'll be arriving in Destiny, Colorado, tomorrow."

Trollinger gave him the rest of the details, a burner cell, and a thick wad of cash. She took his hand and sealed the bargain. "If you need me, call the number in the speed dial, Willie."

He'd left the building, glad to be working with Trollinger. Maybe it was a partnership worth continuing. But only after he finished what lay before him.

As his focus returned to the road ahead, he sneered. "I'm coming for you, Carrie."

Chapter Four

Carrie rode into town on the majestic horse. Josh and Jacob rode on either side of her.

She'd fallen in love with horses back when Willie had been pastor at a church in Bronte, Texas. A couple, members of the church, owned a horse ranch. The woman was her Sunday school teacher and had taught her everything she knew about riding.

Bronte had been a longer stop on Willie's trek back and forth across the country. Eight months. She'd turned twelve there. It had been the happiest time of her life. She'd even let herself dream that Willie might actually settle down and stay there. But of course he didn't. In the cover of night, like always, they skipped town.

Since then Carrie never passed an opportunity to be around horses. Unlike people, she could trust them.

"Carrie, I just realized that I never asked you if you like Chinese food," Josh said. "If you don't, we have a diner that serves all kinds of food where we could go to instead of my parents' restaurant."

She turned to him. "I love Chinese food. It's one of my favorites."

Josh wore a Stetson, a black T-shirt, Levis, and boots, the picture-perfect multiracial cowboy. She'd learned on their ride that his father was Japanese, despite owning a Chinese restaurant. His mother was from Missouri, whose ancestry was Italian. The traits from his parents had produced one incredibly good-looking man. Jet-black hair. Dark, inviting eyes. Perfectly muscled body. A smile that had the power to overwhelm a woman.

As they turned off of West Street onto South Street, Jacob pointed
to the building to their right. "That's Uncle Hiro and Aunt Melissa's
place."

She looked up at the sign, which read "Phong's Wok."

"We can hitch our horses here."

"I didn't know any towns still had hitches in business districts,"
she said, looking directly into Jacob's eyes.

Jacob was just as good-looking as Josh but from the opposite side
of the spectrum. Same cowboy gear, but with blue eyes, wavy golden-
brown hair, and a Greek-god body. The one thing they had in
common was the same devastating smile. Unlike Josh, he hadn't
spoken about his parents during the ride. The only thing she'd gleaned
was that Melissa was his mother's sister. Nothing about his father.

They all dismounted and tied their horses' reins to the hitches. She
almost felt like she'd been transported to the past.

She turned around and looked at the park in the center of the
square.

A few people were enjoying their lunches on the lawn. If Jena
hadn't told her about the strange customs in Destiny during their road
trip, she would've thought it like any other sleepy little town. *Like
Bronte, Texas.* Her gut tightened, recalling what had happened there.

But Destiny wasn't like Bronte, or any other town for that matter.
People formed unusual families here. She glanced at one group on a
blanket next to one of the largest trees. One woman with two men.
Both men were holding her hands. A man wearing a sheriff's uniform
walked up to the trio. The lawman bent down and kissed the woman.
Those four were definitely together.

Under another tree was another woman with long auburn hair. She
held a baby in her arms and was surrounded by three cowboys.

Jena had been telling the truth. Destiny wasn't like any other place
on the planet. Jena was in the typical Destiny relationship. She was
married to two men of her own. *One who is my brother.* Matt and
Sean. What were they like? How did two men agree to share a

woman? How did a woman make such a thing work? She had no idea, not that it mattered. Love was something that she couldn't even dream about for herself. In fact, she'd never had anyone that truly cared for her. The closest thing to love she'd ever experienced was Mrs. Kearns in Bronte. But that had ended badly. Willie didn't love her, despite his words. He'd only used her to help con his victims. Her parents were dead. Had they loved her?

Looking back at the happy faces of the families in the park made her heart sink. She had to keep running. Destiny was just a short stop of a long trip that would never end for her.

"What do you think of our town, Carrie?" Josh asked.

"It's beautiful." She glanced over at the statue that was on the southwest corner of the park, just on the other side of the street from Phong's Wok. Several men were covering it in plastic. She saw that several buildings had plastic draped over their storefronts. "Was there some kind of storm?"

"No storm, though in the next few days it might seem like it," Josh said with a grin.

Jacob turned to Josh. "We need to get the plastic up on the restaurant later today or Uncle Hiro and Aunt Melissa will try to do it themselves."

"You're right. After we get the horses back we'll get the job done."

Curiosity got the best of her. "Guys, I still don't know why the whole town is covered in tarps and plastic. What is going on here?"

"In four days, Destiny's Annual Paintball Extravaganza gets underway," Josh said. "Over fifteen hundred participants will descend on the town for several days of gaming."

She smiled. "Sounds fun."

"Have you ever played paintball, Carrie?" he asked.

For some reason, she had no problem answering most of his questions. At least the ones that weren't about her past. "No. I might be too old for that, don't you think?"

"Not at all." Jacob pulled out an apple from his saddlebag, slicing it into three pieces for the horses. "Two of the best players are two women, and both are over eighty years old."

"You've got to be joking. That can't be true."

"But it is," Josh said. "Ethel O'Leary and Gretchen Hollingsworth are on the top of the leader board year after year."

She really would like to meet those women. They sounded a lot like Mrs. Kearns. "Why does the town host the tournament?"

"The proceeds are earmarked for charities chosen by a board of ten of our citizens." Josh smiled. God, how could any woman resist such a smile? "This year's list includes my mom and dad again. They've been selected for the past ten years."

"Do you two play in the tournament?"

"Sometimes, but most years we end up helping or being security," Jacob said.

"How long will you be in town, Carrie?" Josh asked. "Maybe you might want to try your hand at paintball. It's really very fun. I'm sure that Ethel and Gretchen would be happy to give you lessons."

"Not sure," Carrie said, remembering why she was here. *To meet my brother.* She felt her gut tighten. Had coming here been a mistake? When was Jena going to return with her car? *And my red suitcase?* What if Jena had opened the trunk and looked inside the suitcase? *Oh stop it. You know Jena wouldn't be that nosy. Besides, it's locked.*

She brought her hand up to the chain around her neck that held the key.

"How about we head in and get something to eat?" Josh said. "We can give you more on the history of Destiny inside."

"You and your stomach," Jacob said with a laugh. "It rules you too much."

"Hey mister," she teased. "It's not just him who is hungry. I heard your stomach growl during the ride. Besides, I can't wait to try that sesame chicken you two have been talking about."

"Okay. You got me. But I'm more thirsty than hungry."

She liked how well Josh and Jacob got along. Even though they were only cousins, they acted as if they were brothers.

When they walked into Phong's, she noted the exit out the back, like she always did. It was a habit that she would never break. It was a quaint place that could seat about forty customers. On the walls were paintings of pandas and dragons. By the door was a statue of a golden cat with its paw raised in a sign of welcome.

"Let's sit in one of the booths by the window," Jacob said. "That way we can look out."

When he motioned for her to sit with her back to the front door, she felt uneasy but didn't want to make a scene. "I'm a lefty, Jacob. It might be better for you to sit on the inside."

"Sure thing," he said, moving into the booth. "I've always heard that left-handed people are the smartest people in the world."

"You're absolutely right," she said with a grin. She moved next to him and Josh sat in the booth across from them. Since she had an unblocked path to the back exit and could see out the window, she felt a little better about her position. Plus, she would make sure to keep glancing back over her shoulder at the front door. Another old habit, but one that had kept her safe for a very long time.

"Josh, where are your parents?" she asked.

"Probably in the back. I'll go get—"

"There are my two boys." A middle-aged woman with gorgeous dark hair came out from the kitchen. She wore black slacks and a red pullover with the restaurant's name on the side. "And who is this pretty girl?"

"I'm Carrie," she said, taking an instant liking to Josh's mother, who had obviously given her son and nephew their radiant smiles.

"Melissa Phong," his mother said, taking her hands and squeezing them.

Human touch was so foreign to her, but the sweetness of Mrs. Phong somehow put her at ease. "Nice to meet you."

"You kids look starved to death. I'm going to put in an order with your dad for three plates of sesame chicken, eggrolls, and crab puffs. And after you eat that, I have a special surprise. Don't go anywhere. I'll be right back. I can't wait to learn how you three met." Mrs. Phong spun around and headed back into the kitchen.

"Josh, your mom is quite something." She wondered what her own mother might have been like. "I bet your dad is pretty special, too."

"He is very special, and a very hard worker. I am proud of both of them. Mindy and I are very lucky to be their children."

"You have a sister?" That was one detail he hadn't mentioned on the ride.

"She's a couple of years younger than me. She actually just left town for law school. She had been working as the county court reporter and fell in love with the justice system. I'm proud of her, too."

Would Matt be proud of her like Josh was with his sister? How could he be if he ever learned of what had happened while she'd been with Willie? Navigating the troubled waters of this reunion would be difficult. Why had she agreed to come to Destiny with Jena? Because she was so lonely, she craved having a family like Josh and Jacob had, people that had your back no matter what. *That is why.*

Wanting to get her mind settled down, she looked out the window. "What's with the two dragon statues?"

"There's actually four of them," Jacob told her, pointing to the one directly opposite Phong's Wok. "That's the Green Dragon. It has a shamrock on its chest and most around her believe if you touch it you'll have good luck all day long."

"Then right after we finish eating lunch I'm going to get my hands on it. I could use some luck."

"Back in the late 70s, the four statues were commissioned as gifts for New York City's Central Park by the O'Learys and other prominent citizens of Destiny," Josh told her. "But the gift was rejected and the statues were returned. That's when the battle to change the name of our park began."

She grinned. "Don't tell me that it's called Central Park, too."

"But it is, Carrie. There's a grassroots movement in the town to rename the park Destiny Square Park. Dad supports that group. Mom is with the opposition to keep the name the same."

"Why dragons?"

"Patrick O'Leary is the reason," Jacob said. "And speak of the devil, here he comes with his brother and their wife, Ethel."

Ethel O'Leary, the eighty-plus-year-old woman who plays paintball that I want to meet. She turned around in the booth and looked at the entrance to the restaurant.

The woman standing between the two distinguished men had beautiful silver hair and deep blue eyes.

"If that's Ethel, you must be wrong about how old she is. She's absolutely stunning. She must be in her sixties. And those two men can't be much older than her either."

The man on her left had a thick head of gray hair and a smile a mile long. The one on her right was bald with a beard. He, too, had warm eyes and a sweet grin. The trio walked up to her, Josh, and Jacob.

"Were your ears burning, Patrick?" Josh asked.

"Why yes. You've been talking about me with this lovely lady, right?" Patrick's rich tone only added to his charm. He extended his hand to her. "Patrick O'Leary. And you are?"

"Carrie," she said.

"It's about time these two found a pretty girl like you."

Feeling heat fill her cheeks, she said, "We only just met. I'm a friend of Jena's."

"I'm Sam and this is our wife Ethel, Carrie." Something in his blue eyes told her that he understood how she felt. Or was she just hoping he did. She needed an ally to change this conversation around.

She wasn't used to people being so welcoming and open. But playing a role was something *he* had taught her. Pushing down her worry, she put on her best smile. "Nice to meet you."

"If you're a friend of Jena, then I'm sure you must be a sweet young girl, too," Ethel said. "We're so glad you came to Destiny. I hope you stay long enough to play paintball with me. I'm a champion, you know."

"Where are you from, Jena?" Patrick asked innocently.

Innocent or not, his question was something she couldn't answer. She had no real memories to speak of.

Before she could make up some story, Sam said, "Let's leave these three to their lunch, brother. We've intruded enough today."

She looked directly into Sam's eyes. *He does understand.*

"We'd appreciate that, Sam," Jacob said.

She turned to him and saw in Jacob's eyes the same thing she'd seen in Sam's. Understanding. And something else, something she'd never known before. What was it?

She didn't get these people. They were so different. They actually seemed genuine.

"We can all talk later, Sam." Jacob put his arm around her shoulders, making her feel safe.

That's it. That is the other thing in his eyes. He wants to protect me. Never in her life had anyone tried to protect her. She didn't know what to make of all of it.

"I hope to see you on the battlefield, Carrie," Ethel said, and then the charming trio went to a table near the front door.

"Carrie, please forgive Patrick for being so curious," Josh said, letting her know that he, too, was aware of her discomfort. "He's harmless and loves everybody."

"I believe you. Those three are so charming."

"They're one of the best examples of what living in Destiny can be like," he said. "And here are two more. Here comes Mom with Dad."

"Carrie, this is my husband, Hiro Phong." Melissa placed plates in front of Josh and Jacob. "This is Carrie, Hiro. The young woman I told you about."

"I'm very pleased to meet you." Hiro placed a plate piled twice as high as either of the other two plates. "I made this special for you, young lady." He grinned, making her wonder if he, too, had a part in Josh and Jacob's smiles. "She is as beautiful as you said, sweetheart."

Carrie felt her face warm, letting her know that her cheeks were turning red. "Thank you so much. It smells delicious, but I'm not sure I can eat all of it."

"Don't worry, sweetheart," Melissa said. "We'll pack up the rest for you to take with you."

"Thank you. You both are so very kind," Carrie said, though not sure where she would be able to store any leftovers. She wasn't even sure where she'd be staying tonight, or when she would finally get to meet her brother, which was the only reason she'd come to Destiny in the first place.

"Honey, I have a surprise for you." Jena's voice came from the entrance of the restaurant, which was still to her back.

Carrie swung around, realizing she hadn't kept tabs on the front entrance like she normally would. Why? Because Josh and Jacob's company had put her so at ease.

Not good. Keep your guard up.

But her self-recrimination faded the moment she spotted Jena and the two men heading her direction. She instantly recognized the man on Jena's left from the photo.

Matt. My brother.

Despite trying to keep her emotions buried, her heart raced in her chest. She stood, staring directly into her brother's hazel eyes.

When the trio was next to the booth, Jena grabbed Matt's hand with tears streaming down her face. "Honey, I found her. This is Carrie."

"You what?" Matt turned his attention away from his wife to her. For a split second his eyes seemed to widen, but softened quickly.

The memory of him pushing her on the swing returned. The boy of the past had grown into a man over six feet tall. "Carrie? Is that really you?"

"I couldn't believe it either."

"Honey, I never stopped searching for your sister," Jena said. "When I found her in Dallas yesterday, I knew instantly who she was. But to prove it to Carrie, I had Easton fast track a DNA test through the system. There's no doubt. She's your sister."

"And you're my brother." Trembling and unsure what she should do next, Carrie extended her hand to Matt.

He didn't look like a man who often cried, but she saw tears welling in his eyes.

"Oh my God. I thought you were dead." He didn't shake her hand but wrapped his arms around her, pulling her in tight.

She melted into his embrace and sobbed, wishing she had more memories of him.

"Carrie, you're alive. You're really alive."

Chapter Five

Jacob couldn't believe that he had just witnessed such a heartfelt reunion. Carrie was Matt Dixon's sister, who had been believed dead, killed at the age of three years old.

Like most in town, he knew the story of Matt and Sean's survival from the fire in Belco, Mississippi. He admired them greatly. How two young boys could escape a madman's cult would impress anyone. It was a miracle that Matt and Sean were alive.

For all they'd witnessed, it was even more of a miracle they were sane and not in straightjackets. Instead they had turned out to be good men, who were always willing to help others. They were heroes, serving not just the town but also the entire nation on Easton Black's cyber terrorism task force, Shannon's Elite Team.

"Do you remember me?" Sean asked, placing his hand on Carrie's shoulder. "I'm Sean. Sean MacCabe."

"I–I don't. I'm sorry." Her voice shook with obvious strong emotions.

Jacob sensed her defenses returning.

She cleared her throat and smiled. "Sean, you look kind of familiar."

When she folded her arms over her chest, it made him wonder if she was telling the truth. But why did she feel like she needed to lie? From his own experiences, he could think of a million reasons.

"It's no wonder you don't remember." Sean was just as thrilled that Carrie had been located as Matt. "We were all so young and you were the youngest at only three. Matt and I used to play hide and seek with you. You were never good at hiding and we always found you."

"I remember. Weren't you and Matt friends?"

She was fishing for threads of the truth. He was certain she didn't remember Sean.

"Yes, Carrie. That's me." Sean clearly loved hearing her words.

Perhaps that was the reason Carrie lied, to make him feel better. Or was it something else? Something darker?

"How did you survive, Carrie?" Matt asked, holding her hands.

"I don't remember."

The truth. Jacob could see it in her eyes. She definitely had no recollection of her escape. He looked over at Josh, who was as transfixed on this reunion as everyone else in Phong's Wok. He could tell that his cousin, who was more like a brother to him, was attracted to Carrie just as he was. Was Josh also sensing the storm of doubt and fear blowing beneath her false calm? When he caught his cousin's glance, he knew Josh could.

Aunt Melissa and Uncle Hiro wiped their eyes and stayed fixed in place near the booth. The full attention of every customer was on Carrie and Matt.

Jena turned to her two husbands. "Let's take Carrie back home and get her settled in."

Matt kissed Jena. "Thank you, sweetheart. I thought Sean and my surprise was good, but you blew ours out of the water bringing Carrie to me."

Jena's eyebrows rose. "What surprise?"

"Might as well tell her," Sean said to Matt. "You blew it mentioning the surprise already."

Matt laughed. "I guess I did. Honey, we bought horses for you, Kimmie, and your mom."

Jena smiled. "You didn't?"

"We did. Sean and I got two for us, too. Did you notice the three horses outside? The paint is yours, baby."

"We rode them in with Carrie." Josh clearly had enjoyed their time with her. "I was so worried we were going to ruin your husbands' surprise when you drove up today."

"You mean that pretty paint is mine?" Jena's excitement was obvious to all. "I want to go see her now."

"Then let's go." Matt had been very excited about surprising his wife and was clearly anxious for her to see her gift. "Jacob and Josh, do you mind coming with us?"

"Not at all." Jacob also couldn't wait to see what Jena thought of the mare.

"She's a wonderful horse." Carrie's eyes lit up as they all headed out the door. "Very gentle. You're going to love her."

"She's beautiful." Jena walked up to the paint and began petting her. "What's her name?"

"Her registered name is Queen of Red River Mountain, but you can call her whatever you want to, honey," Sean said. "She's yours."

"Does she have a name her former owner called her?" Jena asked. "Jacob, don't horses usually know their names by her age?"

Jacob appreciated Jena's concern for her new horse. "Don't worry about that. If you pick a new name for her, she'll learn it quickly."

"I'd rather get to know her better before I name her. Besides, I don't have any clue what to call her right now."

Carrie came up beside Jena, looking more relaxed than she'd been earlier. She rubbed the paint's side. "Why don't you ride her first? Maybe a name will come to you."

Being around horses seemed to ease Carrie's anxieties. Jacob experienced the same thing with the beautiful creatures. During his first visits to Destiny, he fell in love with horses because of his own darkness. Recalling his own troubled childhood, he wondered what demons from Carrie's past still haunted her.

"Carrie, I can't wait to ride her, but first, I want to take you home to meet our daughter Kimmie and my mom."

"Don't worry about the horses," Josh said. "Jacob and I will take them back to Stone Ranch. They'll be there when you're ready to ride."

"Do you have another horse for Carrie to ride?" Matt asked. "I would love the entire family to go for a ride soon."

Jacob saw Carrie's face light up at Matt's words. "We'll make sure there's a horse for her, too."

Carrie looked at him and Josh. "Thank you for the wonderful ride today, guys. It was the most fun I've had in a very long time."

"Our pleasure." Josh tipped his hat to her. "Anytime you want to ride again, just let us know."

"Shall we?" Jena asked, motioning to the car she and Carrie had arrived in earlier at Stone Ranch.

"Yes, sweetheart." Matt opened his car door. "Sean and I will meet you two at the house."

Jena passed the keys to Carrie.

Jacob watched the four of them drive away in the two vehicles.

"Are you thinking what I'm thinking?" Josh asked.

"And that would be what exactly?"

"I like Carrie, Jacob. I really want to help her. I can tell that something is not quite right for her, but I can't figure it out."

"I'm with you, bro. There's one person you sent me to when I was struggling with my past."

"Sam O'Leary."

"Yes. He helped me, and I'm betting he can help her, too."

Josh nodded. "Then let's go talk to him."

Back inside the restaurant, they walked to the O'Learys' table.

"Do you mind if we join you for a moment?" Josh asked.

"Please," Sean said.

Ethel smiled. "That was the most touching moment I've ever seen. And that's saying a lot, since I'm 80-something years old."

Patrick laughed. "Sweetheart, you don't have to say 80-something. Sam and I know exactly how old you are." He grabbed her hand. "And you're more beautiful than the day we married you."

Sam took her other hand. "Never more true words have ever been spoken."

The sweet woman's smile broadened. "My mother told me to be wary of Irish men's blarney. I'm glad I didn't listen to her." Ethel kissed her husbands on the cheeks and then turned her attention back to him and Josh. "I'm so glad I got to witness Matt's reunion with his sister."

"It was touching, but I'm worried about Carrie," he told the O'Learys. "And Sam, we want you to talk to her."

Sam leaned forward. "*We?* You mean you and Josh?

"Yes."

Sam smiled. "I thought so. You two are smitten with the pretty lass, aren't you?"

"I sure am." Josh's admission was no surprise. "And I can tell Jacob is, too. Right?"

"Definitely." The truth was he had never been this attracted to any woman before.

"Good for you, boys." Ethel patted his and Josh's hands. "I just love performing weddings."

"Honey, don't get ahead of yourself." Sam raised his eyebrows. "They only just met the girl."

"I know what I know." She kissed him again. "And you know it, too."

"That I do. You picked me and Patrick."

"Or did you two pick me?" Ethel teased. "But let's get back to Jacob's request about you talking with Carrie. Like Jacob, I also sensed she was unsettled about something when Matt came in. What about you? You're the psychiatrist."

"I did notice something in her demeanor," Sam said. "But I couldn't put my finger on it. Even so, I can't make her come to me. Still, I do have a few tricks up my sleeves. I'm sure I'll be able to help Carrie."

Chapter Six

Sitting at the kitchen table, Carrie still couldn't believe she was in the house of her brother, his wife, and Sean MacCabe, Matt's childhood friend.

Why couldn't she remember Sean? She shouldn't have lied but didn't want to hurt him. She also didn't want to let on that most of her memories were gone. Not just when she was three, but also many years after. There were entire blanks that consumed most of her guilty past. But since escaping Willie, all her current memories had remained intact.

With Jena's help she'd found her brother and one buried memory suddenly had surfaced. Was she ready to face more memories? No.

"You were playing with matches that day, Carrie," the bastard had told her time and time again. "Lots of people died because of you, including your parents. Your mother and father are dead because of that fire you started. Did you do it intentionally because they didn't want you?"

Her answer had always been the same, screaming, "Of course I couldn't do such a monstrous thing on purpose. I loved my parents."

Then the slap came, stinging her face, followed by his cruel words. "But they didn't love you, and you wanted revenge. Say it, Carrie. Say you did it on purpose. Tell the truth."

More slaps from the bastard connected until she finally did repeat his exact words. "I did it on purpose."

How can Matt forgive me for what I've done? Why does he even want me here?

"I can't wait for Mom and Kimmie to come back from the Knight's house so they can meet you." Jena's mother had left a note they'd found when they'd arrived. Apparently Jena's mom and daughter had gone to visit Megan Knight, who had a new baby. "I just didn't want to tell them over the phone. And they shouldn't be gone long. I want to see their faces when they see you for the first time. Mom knew how hard I was looking for you."

"Mom was in on this operation, too?" Matt grinned.

"Of course. I had to talk to somebody about it." Jena kissed him.

"Why didn't you tell me?" Sean asked. "I could've helped you with the search."

"I love you, honey, but I know how well you keep secrets."

He hugged Jena. "I'm trained CIA. I do know how to keep a secret."

"From Matt? I don't think so."

They kissed.

Carrie was beginning to believe a relationship with two men and one woman could work. It definitely did with these three. How? What held them together so tightly? What was their bond? Could it be that thing she'd always dreamed about but had never known? Love?

Will I ever find love like theirs? No. I don't deserve it.

"Carrie, would you like some coffee?" Jena asked her. "We also have tea, juice and sodas."

"Honey, this celebration calls for champagne." Sean walked to the wine fridge.

"Nothing else will suffice." Matt nodded, smiling. "Carrie has come back to us. My God, I still can't get over it." He gently placed his hand on her. "You're here. My little sister. I'll never forget this day."

"Me either." As hard as she'd tried to keep her tears from falling, they rolled down her cheeks as her familiar remorse consumed her. "But how can you forgive me so easily?"

Matt put his arms around her. "Forgive you? What do I have to forgive you for?"

She choked out the awful truth. "For killing our parents."

"What are you talking about, Carrie? You didn't kill anybody."

He doesn't know. "I started the fire. I was playing with matches."

"Who told you that lie?" Sean asked.

"Brother Willie told me everything. He told me that our parents didn't love me so I set the fire on purpose."

"That bastard," Matt growled. "He lied to you, Carrie, like he lied to everyone, including our parents. That's not what happened at all."

"It's not? He's told me that my whole life." Realization rolled through her that Willie had been twisting the truth to manipulate her. "But he also always told me you didn't even exist, that you were a figment of my imagination. I never believed him about that. I knew in my heart you were real, Matt."

"I am real. And so are you."

Sean looked her in the eyes. "You didn't kill your parents or mine. Willie did."

Jena came up beside her and took her hand. "I can't imagine what kind of life you had to live with that monster."

"Where is Willie?" Matt said. "I want to get my hands on him."

"I don't know. It's been thirteen years since I've seen him. I ran away from him after so many beatings when I turned sixteen. He always said he was preparing me to be his wife."

"I will kill that bastard if I ever see him again." Matt's tone left no doubt that he meant it. He pulled her in even tighter. "I'm so sorry, but there are no words to tell you how I really feel."

For the very first time in her life, she felt surrounded by people who truly cared for her and wanted to protect her. More tears—cleansing tears—fell, washing away the false guilt that Willie had planted in her mind.

"What really did happen?" she asked them.

"Willie was the leader of a cult in Belco, Mississippi," Sean told her. "I was born in the commune. My parents were with the asshole from the very beginning."

"Our parents came later," Matt said. "Two years before the FBI came."

"FBI? Why did they come?"

"Willie had been stockpiling weapons and was warned to stop. But he didn't. He claimed to be the embodiment of God on earth. As kids, we had to kneel to him whenever he came in the room."

"He always made me do the same whenever we were at home alone," she told them.

"Motherfucker." Matt's face darkened.

"Honey, it's not your fault," Jena said, touching him. "It's Willie's."

Matt sighed, his eyes full of pain, something Carrie knew more about than she cared to. "You were only three."

Sean squeezed Matt's shoulder. "The FBI came. Willie ordered the adults to start firing on them. Everyone, including our parents, were so brainwashed by that bastard they would do anything he said. Carrie, Matt and I always thought we were the only survivors besides Willie. When the shooting started, we ran into his office."

Even though Sean kept his tone soft and his voice steady, Carrie could see in his gray eyes a deep, abiding pain.

"They were only five when the fire happened," Jena said, obviously having heard the horrific story before.

"The asshole was gone," Sean added. "At first, we thought he'd vanished back into heaven. The damn lying fucker had brainwashed all of us. As the smoke got thicker and thicker, Matt found the trap door to a secret tunnel. That's where we knew Willie had escaped."

Matt closed his eyes. "I couldn't find you, Carrie. I looked but you were nowhere to be found. I had no idea that monster took you with him through the trap door."

"It's okay, buddy," Sean said. "She's with us now."

Matt nodded but didn't speak again. It was clear he was trying to contain overwhelming emotions.

"We went back into the main sanctuary, where the other children and adults were. We thought we could lead everyone to the escape route we'd found. But all the adults, including my parents and yours and Matt's, turned their guns on the children and then each other."

The shocking story caused her entire body to shake. "Oh my God."

"My dad spotted me and aimed his gun at my head. That's when some of the women set fire to the drapes using gasoline." Sean sighed. "A spark hit my dad's shirt before he could fire his gun. Matt and I ran back to Willie's office and scrambled down the tunnel. The FBI found us in a field about a mile from the compound. They thought that the only survivors were us and Willie. The bastard was never found. The authorities have continued hunting him without success."

With tears running down her face, Jena said, "Thirty-seven adults died. And for years it was believed twelve children did, too. But one of the twelve survived, Carrie. You."

"Carrie, you didn't start the fire," Matt said. "You weren't even there. You were in the tunnel by the time the flames were roaring."

"I believe you," she said. "You have no idea how this makes me feel. A very heavy weight has been lifted off my shoulders. Willie lied to me, filling in blanks that I couldn't remember."

"You were only three, Carrie," Matt told her. "How could you remember?"

"I remember the smoke."

Chapter Seven

Carrie sipped the delicious coffee that Jena's mother Janet had brewed for her.

"How about I make us some bacon and eggs for breakfast, Carrie?" Janet sat across from her at the kitchen table.

"Thanks, but I had a bowl of cereal with Kimmie before Jena took her to school this morning."

"I can't believe I slept in so late." Jena's mom was a very sweet woman, and quite attractive, too.

"Everyone but Kimmie was up past two. No wonder."

Janet smiled. "How could any of us go to bed early? My sweet Jena found you. You're family, Carrie. In fact, I hope you will call me 'mom' like your brother and Sean do."

Tears welled in her eyes. "I've never remembered my own mother. So for you to include me gives me such happiness that I've never known before."

With a tear rolling down her cheek, Janet reached across the table and grabbed her hand. "You're home, Carrie. Always know you can come to me for anything, anytime."

"I appreciate that so much, but not ever being close to anyone it may be a little hard for me to get used to."

"It will happen faster than you can imagine. Just being in this family and this town has filled so many gaps in my own life. And you'll understand that better when Jena and I tell you about our past. It wasn't easy for us either. We made our share of mistakes, but now we couldn't be happier."

She squeezed the dear woman's hand. "Thank you, Mom."

"Now that wasn't so hard, was it?"

Grinning, she said, "It's a start."

"Good for you. What a wonderful night. Seeing how happy Matt was having you back was incredible. If it hadn't been for Sean's champagne, I doubt I would've been able to sleep at all. I promise that tomorrow I'll make a big breakfast for everyone before they leave for work and school. And for lunch, I'll put something together just for you and me."

Jena, Matt, and Sean had wanted to take some days off but with Shannon's Elite in full alert it wasn't possible. Their skills were required to try to find Cindy Trollinger, a woman who Carrie had learned was very dangerous.

The doorbell rang.

They walked to the front door together.

"Are you expecting anyone?" Having been on the run for so long, Carrie felt a little uneasy.

Janet peered through the peephole. "Oh my God. It's Gary. We had a breakfast date this morning set up. With all the excitement last night I completely forgot." Before opening the door, Janet turned to her. "Don't worry. I'll just cancel. Gary will understand." She swung the door open.

A handsome, middle-aged man wearing a cowboy hat and boots stood on the porch. "Hi, honey." With no reservations, Gary swept Jena's mom into his arms and gave her a kiss. "And this young lady must be Matt's sister."

Janet nodded. "Gary, this is Carrie."

"Pleased to meet you." She held out her hand.

He smiled. "I'm a hugger." Then he gave her a big squeeze. "The whole town is buzzing about you, Carrie. We are so happy that you've been found."

Carrie wasn't sure how she felt about being the center of attention. She was so used to keeping her life private and off everyone's radar. But in Destiny it seemed that was impossible.

"Gary, I totally forgot about our breakfast date," Janet said. "I'm sorry, but—"

"No buts, sweetheart. I plan on taking you and Carrie to Blues Diner. Alice and her husbands are so proud that the restaurant is back. They plan on having a grand opening soon to show off all the renovations they did after the fire. This week is what they are calling their "soft" opening. Only friends and family. Today's breakfast special is your favorite, honey. Biscuits and gravy."

"Carrie, Alice's husbands make the best gravy you'll ever taste." Janet held Gary's hand. It was clear that these two were in love. "What do you say? Shall we take this cowboy up on his offer?"

"Mom, you go. Enjoy yourself. I'll unpack my clothes while you're gone."

"Okay, Carrie. If that's what you'd like to do. Go ahead and get settled in. Gary and I won't be gone long. All our numbers are listed by the phone in the kitchen. If you need anything, just call."

She gave Jena's mom a hug. "Have a good time."

They left, and she closed the door, turning the lock.

She walked back into the kitchen and the phone rang. How many other homes had landlines in Destiny? She grinned, betting most did. The town in many ways seemed from an earlier era, where people greeted each other on the street with a wave, where honesty was the norm, and families looked out for one another.

The phone rang again. She wondered if she should answer it. What if it was important? It might be Kimmie's school.

"Hello?"

"Hi Carrie. This is Josh."

Images of the good-looking cowboy and his cousin Jacob filled her mind. "Hey, Josh. How are you?"

"Great. Jacob and I were wondering if you would like to go horseback riding and have a picnic with us."

The idea thrilled her. "I would like that very much. When?"

"How about we ride over to your place at eleven?"

Your place? She glanced around the space, starting to believe that she had truly found a home. "That would be great."

"Okay, we'll see you then."

She placed the receiver back on the cradle, remembering that Jena's mom would be back shortly. "I hope she won't mind that I'll be leaving with Josh and Jacob."

The phone rang again.

"Hello?"

"Carrie, Gary and I were wondering if you would like to go fishing with us," Jena's mom said.

"Thank you for asking me, Mom, but actually Josh just called and invited me to go horseback riding with him and Jacob."

"That sounds like fun. Go ahead and enjoy yourself. There are some chocolate chip cookies that I made yesterday. Take them with you for those boys. We'll see you around dinner time?"

"They are planning to take me on a picnic lunch, but I'm sure I'll be back by then."

"Ask them to come to dinner, Carrie. We can have a barbeque. It'll be another party celebrating your return."

She smiled, "Mom, how many parties do you plan on throwing on my behalf?"

"Honey, you live in Destiny now. We love parties. You'll find out."

They ended their call, and Carrie finished her coffee. What a turn her life had taken. She had found her brother and gained a sister in Jena, another brother in Sean, a mother in Janet, and a niece in Kimmie. She was about to go on a real date with two handsome men. Could life get any better? She was really happy for the first time. The feeling was so foreign to her, but now that she'd experienced it she didn't want it to end.

She turned off the coffee pot and washed hers and Janet's cups. It felt so good to be at ease, not having to look over her shoulder all the time.

She walked back to the bedroom, recalling what Matt had said last night.

"This is your room, Carrie. As long as you want it, and I hope that's from now on."

The bedroom was light and airy, with soft touches of blue and green and hints of a pale yellow. She'd never stayed in a place long enough to decorate, but somehow her new family had designed this room to her exact taste. She wouldn't change a thing.

Next to the big comfy bed was her red suitcase. Seeing it made her heart skip several beats and her gut tighten. How was she going to tell all of them what was inside?

She lifted it and placed it on the mattress. She took off the chain around her neck. Dangling from it was the key to the suitcase. She unlocked and opened it, seeing the few clothes she owned on the top.

She removed them and hung them in the walk-in closet, which was luxurious. All her things—three pairs of jeans, five tops, her one dress, and two pairs of shoes—didn't even take up a tenth of the space. After putting the rest of her personal belongings in the en suite, she remained in complete awe at having such a beautiful bathroom all to herself.

She returned to the red suitcase. It had been her constant companion since escaping Willie. The only thing left inside it was Willie's leather satchel and its contents. She opened the bag and gazed down at the money and Glock. Counting the stacks of hundred dollar bills, as she always did, she breathed a sigh of relief. There were twenty of them. Ten thousand each. Two million dollars.

Doubt flooded her entire being. Would Matt understand? Jena, Sean and Janet?

Deep down Carrie believed they would, but she needed time to figure out how and when to tell them. They'd just met. A few more days when she got to know them better would make it easier. Once they heard her whole story perhaps they could help her.

She shut the suitcase, locked it, and then placed it in the back of the closet.

Looking at the time on the clock by her bed, she realized that Josh and Jacob would be arriving in an hour. She rushed back to the bathroom to get ready for her date.

Chapter Eight

Josh dismounted his horse, Dusty, in Matt and Sean's front yard. He glanced over his shoulder at Jacob, who was riding Pecos. Their two horses had actually saved their lives not long ago. After being attacked by Trollinger's men, he and Jacob had fallen down a cliff. Dusty and Pecos had returned home, alerting the town that they were in trouble.

"You think Carrie will like riding Fancy?" He tied Dusty and the mare's reins to the fence. Fancy was one of the best horses on Stone Ranch.

Securing Pecos next to the other two horses, Jacob answered, "I'm sure she will. You saw how she was with all the horses yesterday. She loves them and loves riding."

"Yeah. Why are you rubbing your hands together, Jacob? Are you nervous?"

"Quite frankly, yes. Aren't you? After all, she is so beautiful. Kind of out of our league, don't you think?"

"You're talking about Fancy or Carrie?" He laughed.

"Carrie, of course."

"Yes, I'm nervous, too. But I'm also excited. I want to get to know Carrie more."

"Me, too."

They marched up to the front door side by side and rang the bell.

The door opened, and Carrie stood in front of them, a vision of utter beauty. Seeing her blew him away. She wore her hair in a ponytail, and had on a pale green top and nice-fitting jeans. Her hourglass figure was absolute perfection to him.

"Hi guys." She smiled and held out a container. "Chocolate-chip cookies for our picnic, thanks to Janet."

"That will go excellent with what we made you," Jacob said. "I hope you like fried chicken, Carrie."

"It's one of my favorite meals." She grinned. "Which one of you is the cook?"

"Actually we both are." Josh gazed into her gorgeous, golden brown eyes. "You can't be a Phong without knowing your way around a kitchen."

"Let's get on our way," Jacob said. "The place we picked out for our picnic is about an hour's ride away. I'm sure we'll all have quite the appetite by then."

They led her to the horses.

"This is Dusty," he told her, "the best horse I've ever owned."

She smiled. "I've always loved quarter horses."

"That's good to know, since my horse is the same breed." Jacob put his arm around Carrie. "This is Pecos."

"He looks like he's got quite the spirit."

"He sure does," Jacob said with pride.

"And this is the horse you're riding today," Josh told her, leading her to the mare. "This is Fancy."

"Hi Fancy. Aren't you gorgeous?" Carrie rubbed her nose.

The mare responded with a neigh.

Carrie smiled and jumped into the saddle. "Seems like Fancy is ready to go."

"Then let's not keep her waiting." He got on top of Dusty.

Jacob nodded, and mounted Pecos. "Let's ride."

The ride to the spot he and Jacob had chosen was incredible, all because of Carrie. She told them about how Jena had found her in Dallas and how shocked she'd been to learn her brother was alive. When she mentioned what her life had been like with the man named Willie, Josh felt a deep rage growing inside his body for what the lying bastard had done to Carrie. As he glanced at Jacob, he could tell his cousin was having the same reaction. But when she began talking about how glad she was to be in Destiny with her new family, his and Jacob's spirits were lifted. Carrie had suffered so much her entire life. She deserved happiness, and he vowed to do whatever he could to make sure she got it.

"We're here," Jacob said, as they came to the place where the picnic was going to be.

Tall trees surrounded the crystal-clear mountain stream. It was one of the prettiest spots in all of Swanson County.

"Oh my God." She dismounted Fancy. "This is even more beautiful than the ride yesterday."

He tied up the horses and walked next to her, while Jacob spread out the blanket for their picnic.

"Guys, can we walk over to the water before we eat? I want to put my feet in."

"Mountain streams are really cold," Jacob told her. "Are you sure?"

She grinned. "I'm sure. At least for a minute. I've just got to feel it. That way it will help me remember this wonderful day."

He put his arm around her, enjoying the closeness of their bodies. "We can do anything you like."

"If Carrie is doing it, so am I." Jacob pulled off his boots.

"Me, too," he said, taking off his own.

They all three walked down to the stream's edge and stepped in.

"O–hh m–my," she stuttered. "You weren't kidding. It's very cold. Just like ice water."

Jacob took her hand and laughed. "That's because we're not far from the top where the snow melts."

"I tried to tell you, Carrie." Josh believed this day was probably the best he'd ever had. *And it's only just beginning.*

"Well I did say for only a minute." And without another word, she got out.

"Thank God," Jacob said, moving next to her. "My feet are freezing."

Josh jumped out of the water. "Let's go eat. That'll warm us up."

"Last one to the blanket has to clean up." Carrie smiled and then raced to their picnic.

He and Jacob chased after her, but let her win. They didn't intend for her to do anything but have a good time.

They all fell to the blanket, laughing.

"My feet are still freezing," she said. "I'm not sure they will ever be warm again."

"We can help with that," he told her. "Can't we, Jacob?"

"You bet we can." His cousin clearly knew what he had in mind. "You're not ticklish, are you?"

She grinned. "No. Well maybe. Honestly, I don't know."

He realized that she must have never had anyone tease her before. "We'll be gentle," he said, taking her left foot. "This is a test. This is only a test." He ran his finger down the center of her foot.

She immediately jumped and started laughing. "I'm ticklish. I love being ticklish."

"Oh you do, huh?" Jacob smiled, and then started tickling her ribs.

She started laughing hysterically, and to keep her in that beautiful state, Josh continued torturing her feet, adding to Jacob's playfulness.

"Stop. Stop." Her giggles came freely. "You both are going to get it."

"Okay, sweetheart." Josh eased up on the tickling. "We'll be gentle."

Jacob nodded, stopping tickling her ribs and grabbing her right foot. "For now, at least."

Holding her left foot, Josh grinned, picturing what it would be like for him and his cousin to take Carrie to Phase Four. He and Jacob enjoyed being two of the club's resident Doms. The BDSM lifestyle was natural to him and a big part of his life. To Jacob, the practice had helped heal some of the pain of his past.

"Mmm. That feels so good. Keep rubbing them like that. That way isn't ticklish."

It was obvious that Carrie was enjoying the foot massage and was beginning to truly relax.

Moving a little up her leg, he enjoyed the feel of her silky skin.

Jacob did the same.

She licked her lips and sighed. "So good. So very good."

Unable to resist, he moved up and pressed his mouth to hers. She wrapped her arms around his neck, pulling him in closer. She tasted sweet and warm. He wanted more of her. Much more.

By the time he finally released her, he could see that Jacob had also moved up beside her.

His cousin touched her on the cheek.

She turned to Jacob. "Two cowboys just for me? Destiny isn't like anywhere else, is it?"

"No, it isn't." Jacob kissed her.

Feeling his cock harden in his jeans, he ran his hand up and down her sides but kept his eyes locked on them, unable to look away. Her skin was warm to the touch and he could see the passion inside her was growing.

Jacob released her, and she turned back to him, her eyes heavy with want.

Josh kissed her again, but this time he didn't hold back his lust, sending his tongue past her sweet lips and into her warm, delicious mouth. As he deepened their kiss even more, he slipped his hand under her top and began caressing her breast.

Carrie moaned. His hot hunger multiplied. He wanted to be inside her, wanted her, needed her. Did she feel the same?

* * * *

Carrie's mind spun with a million thoughts. "Should I let this go on? Is it wrong to want them this much?"

Josh continued devouring her lips, tangling his tongue with hers. Jacob's hands roamed her body with touches that made her temperature rise.

In the past, her infrequent sex had only been to satisfy her body's needs. One-night stands were all she'd ever allowed herself out of necessity. It hadn't been difficult to keep her heart protected. She'd never bedded any man who would be more to her than just a temporary fulfillment, someone she would never see again.

But this was different. What was this? What was this overwhelming feeling Josh and Jacob were bringing out in her? She was out of control. *I want them, God help me. I do.*

She gazed into their eyes. Did they desire her as much as she did them? It was intense, so wonderfully intense.

Jacob ran his hand down her arm. "Carrie, you are so beautiful. I want you so much. More than anything I've ever wanted in my life."

"And I need you." Josh stared at her, continuing to massage her breasts.

"I don't understand this. I've never felt this way before," she confessed. "But I want you both so very much."

Jacob moved his hand down her stomach to the button of her jeans. Slowly, he unfastened it and undid her zipper, coming so very close to her pussy. Closer. Closer. Even closer.

God, I want him to touch me.

Josh removed her top and bra and placed his mouth on her breast, pinching the nipple of the other one. She felt a shiver shake her entire body, and her desire grew. She moaned as the pressure began to build inside her.

"That's it, sweetheart," Jacob said, his commanding tone deep and full of lust. "That's what we want to hear. We want to know how you feel. That way we can give you all the pleasure you desire."

They were completely focused on her, something she'd never experienced before. Knowing that made her want them even more.

When she felt Jacob touch her pussy and Josh swirl his tongue around her taut nipples, uncontrollable moans came out of her and more moisture pooled between her legs.

Burning inside and out, she began unbuttoning Josh's shirt. "I want to feel your body, Josh."

He smiled and took off his shirt, tossing it to the edge of the blanket.

"My God, you are gorgeous." She ran her fingers over his muscled chest and six-pack abs.

Quickly, he removed the rest of his clothes. His naked body was sheer male perfection. His large cock was erect, and she couldn't resist touching it. She ran her fingers up and down his shaft and then circled the head with the tip of her index finger.

He groaned and his eyes widened, letting her know he was enjoying her touch. "Jacob, I want to feel her pussy."

"You're in for a special treat," Jacob said, ripping off his clothes fast. His body was equally muscular as Josh's, like a Greek god. His thick cock was stiff and the head passed his navel, it was so long. "Do you want to touch me, sweetheart?"

She whispered her answer. "Yes."

He smiled and took her hand, guiding it to his dick. She wrapped her hand around it, but was unable to bring the tips of her fingers together.

"Stroke me, Carrie," he commanded, and she obeyed instantly, unable to resist.

Josh started kissing his way down her body, starting with her neck, down to her breasts, slipping to her abdomen, and then finally she could feel his hot breath on her pussy.

She moved her hands up and down Jacob's shaft, watched his eyelids narrow, and heard his breaths deepen.

Josh kissed her pussy, running his tongue through her flesh. "Your pussy is soft and warm, and dripping with sweet cream."

Electricity ran through her body as he kissed her clit. Feeling his lips pressing on the little bundle caused the pressure to expand. Her desire to have them inside her continued to grow and grow, making her insane.

She continued pumping Jacob's cock. "I want to taste you."

Jacob smiled and touched her cheek. "And I want to feel your sweet mouth on my dick."

She turned to the side and twirled her tongue on the tip of his cock. He responded with a big manly groan and wrapped his hands around the back of her head.

"And I want to feel your tight pussy clenching my dick," Jacob said, reaching for his jeans and pulling out a condom.

She swallowed Jacob's cock, tightening her lips around his shaft. He rewarded her with another sexy groan.

Josh moved his body up her frame until the head of his cock was pressing on her swollen folds.

She burned so hot inside with sensations she'd never felt before. The pressure was too much, too powerful. She needed release in the worst way. She continued sucking on Jacob and wrapped her legs around Josh, a silent plea to him.

"I understand, honey," Josh said, his words heavy and hot with hunger. And then he pushed his cock all the way inside her pussy, delivering a powerful shock throughout her body.

Her legs tightened around Josh's frame and her mouth devoured Jacob's cock. As Josh thrust his dick in and out, she felt it scraping against her G-spot.

She was close—so very close. Never had she been consumed by anything so powerful, and by their actions she knew Josh and Jacob were experiencing the same intensity of this moment. She matched every thrust that came from Josh into her pussy, swallowing Jacob's shaft. The three of them were perfectly in sync, matching each other's movements.

Josh sent his dick deeper and faster into her, pushing her to the edge. Control was no longer possible, and the overwhelming sensations inside her exploded into the most powerful release she'd ever experienced. Lines of electricity shot through her body, causing every part of her to shake. Her skin tingled and her insides burned.

Jacob's hot eyes fixed on her. "I'm coming, sweetheart."

She swallowed as much of him as she could, and then felt his seed hit the back of her throat.

He groaned and closed his eyes. "Yes. God. Yes."

Josh's final thrust into her went even deeper than before. "Fuck, yes. So good."

She squeezed tight around his cock and felt him pulse deep inside her body.

Josh and Jacob remained on each side of her, holding her through the breathless moments until her shivers began to subside. *God, I never knew sex could be this good.*

"That was incredible," Josh said, kissing her tenderly.

"I've never experienced anything like it," she confessed.

Jacob stroked her hair. "Us either, sweetheart."

During their two horseback riding dates she'd found them charming, warm, open, and loved their humor. Now, after they'd made love to her she found them irresistible. *What am I going to do?*

Chapter Nine

When Willie saw the bitch ride up on horseback with two cowboys, he took his gun out of the glove box. But since Carrie wasn't alone it was best to stay put until the men were gone.

Damn. He blew out a hot angry breath, feeling completely aggravated. *Be patient, Willie. Things always work out for you. Just wait for the right time.*

Would the two men leave soon? He hadn't seen Matt, Carrie's brother, or Sean—the MacCabe's son—since they were children, but Trollinger's folder had current photos of the two men. Even from this distance he could tell that the cowboy twosome with Carrie weren't Matt or Sean. Who were the two cowboys then? Jealousy bubbled up from deep inside him.

He watched her dismount in front of the house that he'd been staking out. According to the information Trollinger had given him, Matt and Sean lived in the home with a woman they both claimed as their wife. *Polygamists. Why am I not surprised?*

He'd always known the fuckers had survived the fire, despite the authorities keeping their names out of the news. Just as he'd shoved Carrie into the truck fifty yards from the exit of his escape tunnel and a mile from the Belco compound, the two little bastards had climbed out of the hole he and Carrie had just left. He was certain the two boys hadn't seen them. Matt and Sean had emerged coughing and rubbing their eyes as they sped away.

When Willie saw one of the cowboys kiss Carrie, the past melted away in his mind and rage rolled through his body. *She's mine!*

Then the other man did the same, pressing his lips to hers.

Fucking slut! You were meant to be my wife.

It took all his willpower not to jump out of the rental car and start blasting at all three of them. But that wouldn't serve his purpose. He wanted his money. And he wanted Carrie alive. She was his. If she'd been alone, he would've grabbed her. But she wasn't alone.

The two men got back on their horses and Carrie handed them the reins of the beast she'd been riding.

Here comes my chance after all these years of searching for you.

A middle-aged woman and a young girl walked up the sidewalk to Carrie as the two men rode away. The three hugged each other and he saw the broad smile spread across Carrie's face. Was the little girl Matt's daughter? He couldn't see any family resemblance from this distance but he bet the child was Carrie's niece.

Two women and a little girl. I like those odds.

He grabbed the handle of the car door, and then stiffened as a patrol car turned on to the street up ahead. "This must be your lucky day, Carrie. Our reunion will have to be later. But I'll be back."

He started the engine and headed to his motel in the nearby town to work out how best to get to the woman who had betrayed him.

* * * *

Carrie slid down into the tub. The warm water felt good on her skin. It had been an amazing day. Josh and Jacob were such wonderful men.

She had never felt that kind of closeness with any man in her entire life. After making love with them, she'd enjoyed the delicious meal and wonderful conversation.

It was all too perfect. They were too perfect. She knew better than to let her expectations get out of control. She had to protect herself and her heart.

All the happiness she'd ever known was always short lived. Her mind drifted back to what had happened with Mrs. Kearns when she was a little girl. She'd believed that the dear woman loved her. But of course Willie used Mrs. Kearns's affection for her to his advantage before skipping town. Leaving had devastated Carrie.

Will that happen to me again?

She closed her eyes and licked her lips, thinking about the tender kisses they'd given her before Janet had rushed out the door, inviting them to the barbeque. Josh and Jacob had left to take the horses back to Stone Ranch, but had promised to be back in time for dinner.

What if I'm wrong about them?

Was the best course of action to see Josh and Jacob again? They'd already asked her to dinner tomorrow night and also to join them at the paintball festivities coming up. What would they think of her when they learned that most of her memories were gone?

She took a deep breath and slipped her head under the water's surface. What could she offer them? *A woman without memories and a dark past. A woman with two million dollars in a red suitcase that didn't belong to her.*

She came up out of the water, knowing it was best not to get her hopes up. But reuniting with her brother had changed Carrie, and being welcomed into his family with open arms had caused her to let her guard down. Knowing what was best and doing it were two different things entirely. She was dreaming again about the future and about the possibility of finding love.

Am I setting myself up for heartbreak?

"They might not even show tonight. That's the way it's always turned out for me."

Despite what her logical side told her, she couldn't help wish Josh and Jacob would come.

Am I already falling for them? "If I'm honest with myself, I know I am."

* * * *

Jacob brushed Pecos's coat, and looked over at Josh, who was doing the same with Dusty.

Emmett Stone entered the barn. "Hey, fellas. How did the date with Matt's sister go?"

Josh smiled. "Fantastic. Carrie is wonderful."

"Don't forget beautiful and smart." Jacob had never had a better day in his life. He could tell that his cousin felt the same way.

"So let me see if I get this right. You had a good time?" Emmett laughed. "It sounds like two of Phase Four's resident Doms have been struck by cupid's arrow."

"I can't stop thinking about her, if that's what you're saying," Josh confessed.

"Me either," Jacob admitted. "Our date with her was unbelievable. I can't wait to spend more time with her."

"So glad to hear that, and I'm sure my wife will be, too." Emmett grinned. "Amber and her sister are meeting with all the women in town. After paintball is over, they want to throw a good old-fashioned Destiny welcome party for Carrie."

"Hopefully she's ready for that by then." Though the date had gone perfectly, Jacob still sensed Carrie's reluctance at meeting people at the diner. "Amber and all the ladies might need to check with Jena first. I believe Carrie feels a little overwhelmed, especially because she's been on her own for so long without any family."

"Em, he's right about that," Josh said. "She just needs a little more time to get adjusted."

"I'll let Amber know, fellas. When are you going to see Carrie again?"

Jacob continued brushing Pecos. "Jena's mom invited us over for a barbeque tonight."

"Tonight? What time?"

"Seven."

Emmett looked at his watch. "It is five past six now. You two better get going. I'll finish up with the horses."

"Thanks," Josh said.

Emmett and his two brothers, Cody and Bryant, were some of the best men Jacob had ever known. "We appreciate this, Em."

"Don't give it another thought." Emmett took the brush from him and smiled. "Don't want to show up smelling like a barn now do you?"

* * * *

Carrie helped Janet and Jena make the sides for the barbeque, which had turned into a full-on family celebration. Matt, Sean, and Kimmie were out back. The guys were grilling the meat, and Kimmie was playing with her white toy poodle, Happiness.

Janet peered into the oven. "The pies are about done. Another five minutes."

Jena got out her seven-layer salad. "Mom, we have enough food for fifty people."

"Our guys have big appetites, honey, and you've seen how much Gary can put away in one sitting."

"No more than my two," Jena said.

"And since Carrie's two guys are coming, I want to make sure we don't run out."

"Mom, you've got to stop," Carrie said with a laugh. "Like I told you before, I've only been on one date with Josh and Jacob."

"I count that first horseback ride when you got to town and Jena had to go to TBK for the Trollinger issue as date one. Today was date two. Tonight is date three."

Jena laughed. "Don't even try, Carrie. Mom's loves matchmaking."

Carrie shrugged and turned to Janet. "What about you and Gary? When are we going to hear the wedding bells for you two?"

The woman blushed. "The pies are burning."

"She's good at changing the subject, too," Jena said.

"I hope they aren't ruined," Janet said, bending down and opening the oven door.

"I've never eaten a burnt pie of yours in my life, Mom. Come on." Jena shook her head. "See, Carrie? She did it to me again. Subject change master."

Carrie grinned, slicing the homemade bread Janet had made earlier.

"Honey, how's the search for Cindy Trollinger going?" Janet asked Jena. "Is she still in Denver?"

"She was. A security camera at one of the banks got her image. I was able to discover another alias Trollinger is using. Brenda Dunn."

"If she's that close, has the sheriff considered closing down the paintball games?" Janet sighed. "Who knows what more horrible things she's capable of? But we do know she blames the entire town for her brother's death and wants revenge."

"Mom, Trollinger is no longer in Denver," Jena said. "She boarded a plane in Chicago for London using her new alias just this morning. Sheriff Wolfe is part of Shannon's Elite and is updated on all our findings. Even though Trollinger is out of the country, he still plans on beefing up security."

"London?" Janet wiped off the counters. "That woman sure gets around, doesn't she?"

"Who was her brother?" Carrie asked, seeing the concern in Jena and Janet's eyes.

"Kip Lunceford," Jena told her. "A criminal mastermind that once worked for TBK. He always hated the two brothers who started the company. A complete psychopath and egomaniac. He was responsible for so much heartache in our town. Lunceford worked with Russian mobsters, who ended up murdering Charlie Blake, one of Destiny's deputy sheriffs, leaving Ashley, Charlie's wife, to raise their two kids alone."

"And don't forget Shannon Day also lost her life," Janet said. "The woman who your team is named after."

Carrie thought there were similarities between this Lunceford man and Willie. Though Willie had never taken a life, as far as she knew, she had no doubt he would have no qualms killing if he thought it would benefit him. "And Lunceford's sister is just as dangerous?"

Jena nodded. "Maybe more so."

"What happened to Lunceford?" Carrie asked.

"Kip was finally killed here by Jaris Simmons after the bastard tried to run another of his deadly schemes." Jena walked to the refrigerator. "That's why Cindy Trollinger is after revenge."

"But enough about that topic," Janet said. "Today is about Carrie. This is a party."

Carrie glanced at the clock on the wall. "Shall we start carrying the food to the backyard? I expect that Gary, Josh, and Jacob should be here any moment." *If Josh and Jacob show at all.*

The doorbell rang.

"Are you psychic, Carrie?" Janet said, smiling.

"Hardly. I just knew we were running out of time." Excitement rolled through her. They had come after all.

"We'll have extra hands to help us," Janet said, and then headed to the front door.

"Mom sure does love throwing parties. You're lucky she didn't invite the whole town, but don't be surprised if that happens in the next few days."

"I'm still getting my bearings, so I'm glad it's just us tonight."

Janet returned with Josh and Jacob, who were both carrying a bottle of wine.

Seeing them again made Carrie so happy. She couldn't stop smiling. They looked so handsome.

They actually showed up.

"Hi Carrie." Josh came over and gave her a sweet hug.

"Hi."

Jacob kissed her on the cheek. "Hey, you."

"Hey."

"Boys, help us carry this food out," Janet said. "Gary should be here any minute, and we want to eat while everything is still hot."

They all headed to the backyard, where the picnic table had already been set with the dishes and silverware. A sign hung from the branches of the tree above the table with writing that clearly was Kimmie's. "Welcome home, Aunt Carrie."

The little girl ran up to her with Happiness by her side. "Did you see what I wrote, Aunt Carrie? Daddy Matt helped me write it and Daddy Sean hung it in the tree for me."

She bent down and gave her niece a hug. "Thank you, sweetheart. I love it."

"And I love you," Kimmie said before running back to the center of the lawn to play with her dog.

Carrie turned to Jena and Janet. "Did you all hear what Kimmie said to me?" She felt her eyes fill with happy tears. "She said she loved me. No one has ever said that to me before."

Jena gave her a hug. "We all love you, Carrie. We love you very much."

"Of course we love you," Janet said. "We will never stop loving you. You're our family. Forever."

Josh put his arm around her. "Seems like you've found your home."

Jacob squeezed her hand. "And you couldn't have a better one, Carrie."

"I believe you." Needing to keep busy so as not to start sobbing, she said, "There's more food inside, guys. Will you help me with it?"

"Absolutely."

As Janet and Jena arranged the plates of food, Carrie walked back into the house with Josh and Jacob for the rest of the sides.

The doorbell rang.

"That's got to be Gary, guys." She walked into the entry and opened the door.

Gary stood there, carrying a dozen red roses.

"Oh Gary," she said. "Janet is going to love them."

"She's definitely crazy about flowers. I make sure to bring her some at least once a week."

"You better hurry up and give them to her," Jacob said, moving next to Carrie. "Janet's in a hurry to get the meal underway."

When they went out the back door, Janet looked up. "Gary, you sentimental sweetheart." She took the roses. "They are beautiful. Thank you, honey."

When they kissed, Carrie knew these two were meant for one another. No doubt about it. She glanced over at Josh and Jacob, who had joined Matt and Sean at the grill.

"Everyone take a seat," Janet said. "I'm going inside to get a vase and will be right back. These gorgeous roses that Gary brought me will be the centerpiece for our meal."

As instructed, everyone moved to the table. Carrie sat down first. Josh and Jacob came next, sitting on either side of her. The rest settled down into their seats.

The laughter and joy around the table of delicious food was another first for her. It was almost surreal. She looked from face to face at her newfound family. Kimmie sat between Janet and Gary, who were looking at each other like two love-struck school kids. Jena sat between Matt and Sean, smiling broadly. She turned to Josh and then to Jacob. They put her at ease from the moment she'd met them, and now she was completely relaxed being with them.

This has been the most wonderful day of my life.

Janet stood. "Okay, who is ready for pie? We have apple and cherry."

"And don't forget that we made homemade ice cream to go with it, Mom," Jena said.

She helped get the pie sliced and plated. Suddenly, she thought about her red suitcase up in the closet. In her heart she knew they would all understand. Josh and Jacob had proven to Carrie that they already cared for her. Her brother Matt had the heart of a lion and would protect her no matter what. Sean, too, who was just as much like a brother to her as Matt, would always have her back. Jena had shown what lengths she would go to for those she cared about. She'd been the one who had found her. And Janet had asked her to call her "Mom."

And Kimmie said she loved me.

Chapter Ten

Josh loved having his arm around Carrie, looking up at the first stars appearing in the sky. She sat between him and Jacob on her family's front porch swing. There wasn't any place in the world Josh would rather be than right here.

Jena and Janet had ordered him and Jacob to keep her out of the kitchen, saying they would handle the cleanup with their guys. It was Carrie's party after all.

The breeze was still warm, though the sun had set thirty minutes ago. He had enjoyed spending time with Carrie at her family's barbeque. The more he got to know her, the more enamored he became. And their date today had blown him away completely. He'd never enjoyed anything as much as their picnic. Carrie was playful and adventurous. Smart and gorgeous. Genuine and caring. No woman had ever had such an impact on him before. The sex had been vanilla and yet so incredible. He loved every one of her curves and the feel of her silky skin.

He sensed she had a submissive streak inside her that he would love to dominate if given the chance, but they were just at the very beginning. Even though everything inside him wanted to dive in head first, he believed it was best to take this nice and slow with Carrie.

He grabbed her hand and squeezed. "I hope you enjoyed our date today."

She squeezed back. "It was wonderful. Thank you."

Jacob took her other hand. "Josh and I came up with another plan."

She grinned, looking more beautiful than ever. "Oh you did, did you?"

"We did," Josh said. "Did I tell you I'm a pilot?"

"You did. You work for TBK, besides helping out at your parent's restaurant."

"My bosses, Eric and Scott Knight, agreed to let me take the company plane tomorrow night. Carrie, what do you think about the three of us having dinner in Red River, New Mexico? There's an incredible steakhouse there."

"Oh that would be exciting. I've never been in a plane before."

"Not only will you be in the plane, you're going to sit next to the pilot."

Jacob laughed. "Where does that leave me?"

"You'll be our navigator, buddy."

"I never navigated no planes before, mister," Jacob said in a thick southern accent.

They all laughed.

"It'll only take three minutes to learn," he said. "You'll be great."

"It's a date then," Carrie said, giving them both kisses on the cheek.

They all leaned back in the swing and continued enjoying the evening. Tomorrow would be their second date, one of many more if he had his way. He wanted to spend as much time with Carrie as possible, and he was certain Jacob did also.

"Guys, I can't tell you how different being here in Destiny is for me. It's like another world."

Even though they were having fun, he and Jacob could sense that there was more on her mind, more she was struggling with.

"Carrie, have you ever seen such a night in your life?" he asked, gazing into the heavens, hoping to ease her worries. "There are so many stars out here."

"Only a few times," she answered. "When I lived in Bronte, Texas, as a young girl, a sweet lady who had a porch very much like this one sat with me and taught me about the Big Dipper and Orion's Belt. Until now, it was the happiest time of my life. Mrs. Kearns and her husband owned a horse ranch. That's where I learned to ride and love horses. But as usual, Willie snapped me up out of there."

Josh recalled what she'd told him and Jacob on the horseback ride about the bastard preacher. He couldn't imagine the hell she'd been through having grown up in the happy home of his parents, Hiro and Melissa Phong. But Jacob's childhood had been very different, and no doubt he related to her past.

"Why did he keep moving you around?" Jacob obviously was in tune with her feelings, hoping to get her to open up more to them.

"Willie was a con artist. We only stayed in any one place for a short time so that he never got caught."

Josh stroked her hair. "What kind of schemes, Carrie?"

"He was a thief." She lowered her head as if she was in deep thought. Then after several seconds of silence, she lifted her head.

He could see the tears in her eyes. "What's wrong?"

She sighed. "I'm holding a secret that I need to tell someone."

"You can trust us, sweetheart."

Jacob squeezed her hand. "Whatever it is."

"Ever since I left Willie, I've been carrying a red suitcase. Do you remember how worried I was about it on our first horse ride?" She closed her eyes. "This is harder than I thought."

"Just say it," Jacob urged.

"I just have to blurt it out. One. Two. Three." Her eyes opened. "There's two million dollars of stolen money in that suitcase. It's upstairs in my closet."

"Oh my God, Carrie," Jacob said. "You've been lugging that around since you were sixteen?"

She nodded. "I took it when I escaped Willie. I swear I haven't spent a dime of it. It's all there. I just want to get it back to the rightful owners. I tried once, but that's when Willie nearly caught me. I was scared and didn't know what to do. I still don't."

"First thing you need to do is tell Matt, Sean, and Jena, sweetheart," Josh said, holding her close. "They're CIA. They'll be able to help you."

"I've planned on telling them, but I haven't found the right time."

Matt walked out. "Jena sent me out to see if you three wanted anything to drink. We've got the kitchen cleaned up, and Kimmie put to bed. Mom and Gary left for an evening stroll. Sean just opened a bottle of scotch. We all are ready to relax, if you three would like to join us."

Josh looked Carrie in the eyes. "Seems like the right time is now to tell them."

"Yes it is," she said. "Matt, after you pour the drinks can we all sit down. There's something very important I need to tell you."

* * * *

Glad to have Jacob and Josh next to her on the sofa, Carrie took a sip of the scotch that Sean had poured for everyone. It was liquid courage that she definitely needed right now.

Matt sat next to Jena on the matching sofa opposite theirs. Sean was in the chair by the fireplace.

She was nervous, but was so thankful she finally had this opportunity to come clean about the money.

"Okay, Carrie," Matt said, looking her directly in the eyes. "I'm your big brother. You can tell me anything."

She took a deep breath and closed her eyes. *One. Two. Three.* She opened her eyes. "There's two million dollars of stolen money in my red suitcase."

"Two million dollars of stolen money?" Matt looked shocked. "I know you're not a thief. So where did you get that kind of money? Of course, Willie. Right?"

"Yes."

Jena shook her head. "You've been carrying that money around for thirteen years?"

"Since she was sixteen," Jacob said, putting his arm around her.

"It's a very long story," she said.

"Hold on, Carrie." Sean stood. "Let me get the suitcase first and then you can finish telling us everything." When he returned, he placed it on the coffee table. "It's locked."

She pulled out the chain with the key and unlocked it. She brought out the satchel and placed her Glock and the stacks of cash onto the table.

"Oh my God, Carrie," Jena said. "You could've been killed for that kind of money."

"But at least she's packing," Sean said. "Definitely a member of this family." He opened his coat and revealed his own gun.

"I know it was dangerous, Jena, but I was always very careful. No one ever knew what was in my suitcase."

"Willie knew," Matt said. "I can't even let myself think of what would've happened if that bastard had found you."

"He almost did. That's why I've never been able to return the money to the rightful owners. He was always too close." She told them about how she'd returned to Bronte, hoping to give back the fifty thousand dollars that belonged to the church Mrs. Kearns attended. "I spotted Willie at a rest stop on the highway into town. He had a full beard, and was wearing sunglass and a hat, but I recognized him despite the disguise. I knew he had come back to Bronte to get me. How he'd learned what I was planning, I don't know. Maybe I told someone at the café I was working at. I just don't remember. But I knew it wasn't safe for me to go through with my plan. So I drove through Bronte without stopping and never returned."

"How many churches did Willie steal from?" Jena asked.

"Hundreds. Always the small ones that were struggling." She pulled out the list of the churches she'd kept for all these years. "Congregations with less than fifty members, usually elderly, but with clear title to their property. He would come in and offer to become their pastor for pennies. Matt, do you remember how charismatic he could be?"

"I sure do."

"Once he won their trust he would convince the deacons to take out a loan, saying it would help revitalize the church and bring in new members. Once the money was deposited, Willie would pull it out of the bank and then he and I would move to the next town and next church."

"Bastard hasn't changed one bit," Sean said, his face dark with anger. "Quite the scam."

"I've been searching for Willie for years, Carrie," Matt said. "This new information will help to bring that asshole to justice."

"Honey," Jena said, grabbing Matt's arm. "The stuff I uncovered to find Carrie might also help. Black supported my every step in searching for your sister. I'm sure he'll be more than glad to give us a hand on this, too."

Matt nodded.

Sean said, "I think the first thing we need to do is get this money to TBK so it's more secure."

"Agreed," Matt said. "And tomorrow morning we'll take Carrie to Black and the rest of the team to tell her story. All hands on deck for this one."

Josh pulled her in tight, making her feel safe and protected. "Everything is going to work out fine, sweetheart."

Jacob squeezed her leg. "You've got the best on your side. Shannon's Elite is the best the CIA has to offer."

"And I also have you and Josh to thank for helping me get this off my chest. I've been carrying this around for thirteen years. None of you can imagine what a burden has been lifted off of me. I'm not alone anymore."

"Sis, you will never be alone again," Matt said. "I promise."

Sean took a sip of his drink. "That's a fact, Carrie. You can count on us."

"I found you," Jena said. "You can always come to us for anything. We love you."

Sean put down his glass and started putting the stacks of money back into the satchel. "First things first. Let's get this money out of here."

"The most secure place in the building isn't Shannon's Elite area," Matt said. "It's Eric and Scott's offices."

Sean stood and slung the satchel's strap around his shoulder. "Carrie, it's lovingly referred to as the Presidential Fortress of Solace by the employees. All the churches' money will be safe there."

"We need to call Dylan to let him know we're coming," Matt said. "He's TBK's head of security, Carrie. And he's also part of Shannon's Elite."

"Thank you so much. I just want to make sure that this money gets back to those churches. They are good people. They didn't deserve what Willie did to them."

"Sean and I won't be gone long," Matt said.

"I'm going, too," Jena said, taking the list of churches from her. "I want to put in this information so that we'll have it when the team meets with Carrie."

Matt kissed her. "Good idea, baby."

"Do you mind keeping an eye on Kimmie for us?" Jena asked.

"That little angel. Of course not."

Matt came over and gave her a hug. "I promise you that everything is going to be okay from now on."

"I believe you."

After the trio left with the two million dollars, she leaned back between Josh and Jacob. "That's the first time in thirteen years that money has been away from me."

"How does it feel?" Jacob asked.

"So good. I feel two million dollars lighter." She couldn't stop grinning. "How can I ever repay you? I'm not sure I would've ever found the courage or right time to come clean with my family without your help."

"Coming to dinner with us tomorrow night is a start." Josh pressed his lips to hers. "The date is still on, right?"

"Absolutely."

"Sweetheart, you did good tonight." Jacob kissed her. "A lot of innocent people are going to benefit because of you."

She smiled. "So this is what happiness is all about."

Kimmie's little dog came running, and they all laughed.

* * * *

Parked back on the street to stake out Matt and Sean's house, Willie held his gun. Earlier, he'd lost his mind when he'd seen his bitch with the two fucking cowboys. But now the calm that had gotten him through many a close call was back in place.

He smiled. "No need to rush. I've waited all this time to find her. And now I have a full-proof plan to get my money back and make that bitch pay for what she did to me."

And when he completed Trollinger's task, the amount he would be paid, along with the two million he recovered from Carrie, would give him all he needed to live out his life on an island in the Caribbean, drinking rum and fucking the local beauties to his heart's content. Carrie would be his bitch slave, taking care of all of his needs. By the time he finished with her, she would be grateful to do anything he told her.

He glanced down at the screen of the burner phone Cindy Trollinger had given him in Denver. The e-mail from her had come in less than an hour ago. It had a photo and very detailed instructions. The final line was the agreement he'd made with her for the information about Carrie's whereabouts.

"Kill Jaris Simmons." The man had killed Trollinger's brother.

The photo was a few years old, when Simmons had still been working as a police officer in Chicago. Now he was a deputy in this backwater town and also worked with his wife raising service dogs for the blind. *What a pussy.* Watching the bastard die would be a pleasure.

Willie put the phone away and watched three people, a woman and two men, come out of the house down the block. He brought binoculars to his eyes.

None of them was Carrie. But he was certain she was inside. Once again, not alone. The two cowboys were with her and so was Matt's daughter Kimmie.

Patience, Willie.

The cell rang.

Only one person had the number. "Hello, Cindy."

"Where are we on taking care of that issue we talked about, Reverend?"

He grinned. "You mean killing Simmons?"

She didn't say a word, which let him know she wasn't pleased. Trollinger liked speaking in code, whereas he was more to the point unless he was working a con. That's when it was best to talk around specifics.

"When can I expect the job to be done, Willie?"

"I'm working out the details for both our issues, ma'am. There's a big paintball event that starts day after tomorrow."

"You don't have to school me on anything that happens in Destiny." Trollinger's tone sharpened. "I've been keeping my eyes and ears on that town for a very long time."

He'd learned from the man working the desk at his hotel in the nearby town that Trollinger was the most hated woman around. How was she able to keep tabs so closely here? If she ever set foot in town almost every citizen would recognize her. He bet that she had spies on her payroll. Best to stay on her good side. At least for now.

"Then you know, Cindy, that the big event will bring thousands of visitors to Destiny. That's when I'll make my move. The crowds will give me the cover I need for both our operations."

"Just make sure it gets done, Reverend."

The line went dead, just like Simmons would be very soon.

Chapter Eleven

Getting out of her brother's car, Carrie looked at the nine-story building.

"Welcome to Two Black Knights Enterprises," Jena said.

"Home of Shannon's Elite," Sean added.

TBK's edifice was all glass, but the lower floors were all covered in plastic, like the rest of the places in Destiny. Already, out-of-towners were arriving for the big paintball event that started tomorrow. "It seems this building is too large for this size town."

"Look to your left, sis." Matt pointed at the even larger office building next to TBK. It was ten stories and had a projecting cornice decorated with interlocking stone circles and leafy garlands. "That's O'Leary Global, Destiny's first billionaire family. The Knights are the second. Both companies are headquartered here but have offices around the country and world."

"We better get inside," Sean said. "We still have to process Carrie with Terrence."

"Terrence?"

"Don't worry," Jena said. "He's security and I called ahead to let him know we were bringing you."

They walked into the building.

The man behind the desk had gray hair and a warm smile. "Hello Mrs. Dixon-MacCabe. Mr. Dixon. Mr. MacCabe. And I believe you are Miss Carrie Dixon, correct?"

"I am," she said, realizing that was her real name. Had been her entire life, though Willie had told her otherwise.

"I'm Terrence McCoy. Pleased to meet you, Miss Dixon."

"Me, too," she said, instantly taking a liking to the man. "Please call me Carrie."

"And you call me Terrence." He held out a pen for her to take. "I have a few things for you to fill out."

She couldn't believe all the questions that were on the forms. "You really need to know my weight, Terrence?"

"Protocols. And your height, too, Carrie."

Sean smiled. "Don't mind Terrence. He takes his job seriously."

"Yes, I do, sir."

"Congratulations on your promotion," Jena said. "You deserve it."

Terrence smiled. "Thank you."

"Being Dylan Strange's right-hand man might be tough," Matt said. "But if anyone can do it, it's you."

"Thank you, sir."

"Never will stop with the formalities, will you?" Sean asked.

"You were officers in the Marines. I was enlisted. That will never change."

Carrie hadn't known that her brother and Sean had served in the military. There was so much more she wanted to learn. Thank God, it seemed she would be able to stay in Destiny for a long time to find out. No need to run any more. "All done, Mr. McCoy."

He took the paperwork. "Excellent. Next, I'll need to get your fingerprints and a photo of you."

"Okay," she said, feeling like she was getting ready to join the CIA herself.

There was no ink to take her fingerprints. Instead all she had to do was place her hand on a scanner. And taking the photo had been different, too. Terrence had her walk into a booth. The whole picture-taking process was automated and took several minutes.

Once all the steps were completed, Terrence opened a drawer and brought out a temporary badge. He slid it into a slot that was attached to his computer. Then he handed the badge to her. "You're all set. This will give you all the access you need."

"Thank you, Terrence."

He smiled. "My pleasure, Carrie."

"Let's try your badge," Jena said.

She handed it to her and Jena swiped it on the reader by the glass door that led into the main building.

There was a buzzing sound and Matt opened the door for her.

Having been cleared to enter, Carrie walked out of the lobby and into the main area of TBK with Jena, Matt, and Sean. Two Black Knights Enterprises was very modern and impressive.

They led her to an elevator that had more security measures than she'd ever seen before. "Josh and Jacob were right about this place being the safest in town. Perhaps in the world."

"It is. We have the latest technology available," Matt said. "And the two million is in the most secure area of the entire building, though that's not where we're going."

Sean swiped his card, and the elevator doors opened.

She started to step inside.

"Wait," Matt said. "Everyone that gets into the elevator must use their card."

"Everyone?" She held out the visitor's card that the guard at the front had given her a few moments ago after Matt had vouched for her and signed her in.

"Yes," Jena said. "If the weight in the elevator exceeds the amount it should for the people inside, the doors will shut and not open until Security comes and gets you."

"I thought it was odd that I had to put my weight down on that form. I'm glad I told the truth."

Sean and Matt laughed.

Jena grinned. "A few pounds either way wouldn't have made much of a difference, but it is best to be honest around here."

After they all swiped their cards, they entered the elevator.

Sean punched the button marked B2.

Carrie turned to Jena. "Your CIA team works in the basement?"

"We just moved from our temporary offices to the permanent ones. We're very happy with our new home. Langley had considered trying for our own location, but with TBK's vast security, the top brass thought it better to keep us here. We have the whole floor to ourselves."

When the elevator stopped, the door didn't open immediately. A voice came through a speaker. "This level is secure and requires the highest clearance. Please say your name and access code. Then step forward for a retina scan, placing your chin on the rest and keeping your eyes open."

Carrie felt like she was in a James Bond movie. "That wasn't a normal photo the guard took of me, was it?"

"Correct," Sean said. "He got a complete scan of your eyes."

"I knew it was strange that he made me stay still for so long. What's my access code then?"

"Your birthday, for now. Two digits for the month, day, and year."

"Relax, sis," Matt said. "It's really simple. I'll go first. Matthew Lee Dixon. Alpha-Texas-One-Six-Gamma-Charlie-Seven." He leaned forward as the voice had instructed. She could see a blue light run up and down his face.

"You are cleared, Mr. Dixon. Next."

Sean and Jena went next.

"Your turn," Jena said, taking her hand and squeezing it lightly.

"Carrie Anne Dixon. Ten-Eleven-Eighty-Five." Like the other three, she positioned her chin in the rest and opened her eyes as wide as she could. The light made her blink.

"Sorry, I blinked. Do we have to do it again?"

But the voice let her know the scan had worked perfectly. "You are cleared, Ms. Dixon."

"Everyone blinks," Matt said as the doors opened. "Doesn't matter. The scan happens superfast."

They walked into a room. Two nice-looking men in dark suits stood by a set of glass doors.

"Carrie, this is Brock Grayson and Cooper Ross," Jena said. "Guys, this is Matt's sister Carrie."

They shook hands.

Brock opened the door. "The rest of the team is already in the War Room."

As they followed Brock and Cooper down the hall, she whispered to Jena, "War Room?"

"Not actual wars, but the name definitely fits for the kind of work we do here. We are the very front of the country's war on cyber terrorism."

When they walked into the room, Carrie saw several people seated around a long conference table, which had images floating on its surface. She saw a couple of them typing away on the table's top at what looked to her like touch monitors. Again, she turned to Jena for answers. "That's an impressive table. Are the monitors voice activated as well?"

"Yes." Jena smiled. "That's my baby. I designed it. Each team member can work individually or the entire table can become a single screen that can tie into the monitors on the walls."

She was introduced to the entire Shannon's Elite team. Being more nervous than she'd anticipated, she wished that Josh and Jacob were here to support her. The men and women around Jena's special table were CIA. What would they think of her after she told them about the two million dollars?

"Thank you for coming, Carrie," Easton Black, the team's leader, said. "Everyone take a seat and let's get started."

It didn't take long for her to relax, as each of the team listened intently to her recount how she'd escaped Willie with the two million dollars of stolen money. "I kept a list of each church Willie conned."

"We made copies of Carrie's list," Jena said, passing around the pages to the others. "It's very detailed. I'll have a digital copy up that you can download to your ROCs after this meeting."

"Carrie, how old were you when you started the list?" Jaris Simmons—she'd learned during the introductions—was one of the sheriff's deputies and also the newest member of Shannon's Elite.

"I think around five or six."

"How did you know to do that so young?" the other deputy, Nicole Coleman, asked.

"At first, it was just a journal I started to remember all the places we lived. Then as I got older I realized the information might be valuable someday. We always left each town in such a hurry that by the time I was thirteen I suspected that Willie was robbing from each of the congregations, although I didn't know how he was doing it. It took me a few more years to figure out his whole scheme, but when I did I started planning how I was going to escape and return the money."

Mr. Black nodded. "It's amazing that you have such high ethics having been raised by such a wicked man."

"Actually, from every congregation I met such kind and decent people. I decided at an early age I wanted to be like them."

"Some of those churches likely don't exist anymore, Carrie," Joanne Brown, the woman to Black's right, said.

"Maybe not, but as you can see on the papers that Jena gave you, I do have a name of at least one elder from each church on the list. Will you help me get this money back to its rightful owners?"

"Yes, but not only that, Carrie," Black said, "we're going to find Willie and make sure you don't have to run ever again. Dylan, what can you tell us about the man's last known whereabouts?"

"August of last year he was captured on a security camera at a bank in Wisconsin," Dylan Strange, the head of TBK security as well as Shannon's Elite member, said. Dylan wore sunglasses, even though they were inside and underground. Carrie wasn't quite sure what to make of him, but since he was on the team she thought he had to be one of the good guys.

"Willie had been living there for a few months under an alias," Jaris continued. On another screen a small church appeared. "We knew that he'd been attending the Good Shepherd Chapel while living there. We also know that he had been wooing the members to make him their pastor. What we hadn't known was why." Jaris smiled at her. "But thanks to Carrie, now we do."

"What happened to the church?" Carrie asked, wondering how many other churches Willie had conned after she'd escaped. "Did he steal from them, too?"

"No," Jaris said. "Perhaps without you it was harder for him to convince congregations to take a chance on him."

"I bet you're right, Jaris. Whenever we showed up to a church Willie told them a sob story about how he was trying to raise me on his own and about how my fictional mother had died in a car accident."

Matt grabbed her hand. "I hate that you had to go through so much with that bastard."

"So how do we catch him?" Black asked the team.

"Boss, why don't we have Jena research all the tiny churches that are looking for pastors," Cooper said.

"Make sure they are in small towns, too," Carrie told them. "We never lived in any town with a population over twenty thousand."

"Excellent suggestion, sis," Matt said. "I'm sure he stayed out of the big cities not only to keep from being recognized but also to stay away from bigger law enforcement agencies."

"How long before you can have something to us, Jena?" Black asked.

"I can have it done by midnight tonight. Maybe earlier with Matt and Sean's help."

"Perfect." Black turned to her. "Carrie, you've been an incredible help. I have little doubt that we'll have Willie Mayfield in custody very soon."

"Thank you so much."

Black addressed his team. "Let's take a quick break before we come back for our other business items."

Jena, Matt, and Sean walked back to the elevator with her.

"How did I do?" she asked them, feeling better about the situation.

Sean smiled. "Couldn't you tell you were a hit with everyone?"

"Of course she was," Matt said. "She's my sister."

"And she gave us all we need to track down a guy the FBI has been searching for since the fire in Belco all those years ago."

"Sixteen years to be exact," she said. "I'm sure you have to go back for the rest of your CIA business, so I'll go to Phong's Wok and have some jasmine tea until you're finished."

"Chinese again?" Sean teased. "I know the real reason you're going there. Or should I say the real cowboys you hope to see?"

She grinned. "They might have something to do with it. Plus, it's a beautiful day to walk and enjoy Destiny's Central Park."

Matt grinned. "Be careful who you say that to."

She laughed. "I remember why. The big controversy about the name. I'll be extra careful. I shouldn't get in much trouble, no farther than Phong's is."

"One block is all," Jena said. "When were done here we'll join you. Shouldn't be more than an hour."

"See you later," she said, and punched the elevator button for the main floor. The door closed. Once again she had to go through the security measures. Apparently, TBK and Shannon's Elite wanted to know who left as much as who came.

Chapter Twelve

Carrie entered the Wok and was greeted by Melissa Phong.

"It's so good to see you again, Carrie. I hope you're hungry. The special today is anything you want for free. It's Hiro's and my way of welcoming you to Destiny."

"That's very sweet of you, Mrs. Phong, but I certainly expect to pay."

"Nonsense, my dear, and please call me Melissa." The sweet woman led her to the same booth she'd sat in the other day with Josh and Jacob. "Besides, it is time for my lunch. Would you mind if I joined you? I hate eating alone and that way we could have a nice chat." Melissa poured her a glass of water.

"That would be really nice. I was planning on only having Jasmine tea until Jena, Matt, and Sean arrived, but I am rather hungry. And I don't like eating alone either."

Melissa smiled and her eyes lit up, once again revealing the family trait that both Josh and Jacob shared. "Then it's all settled. I'll go to the kitchen and have Hiro prepare lunch for us. Since you had Chinese recently, would you like something different? Hiro makes an incredible hamburger, though please don't mention that to anyone, especially our friend Lucy."

"Lucy's Burgers? The restaurant on the southeast corner of the square?"

"That's right. Just three doors down from our place. Lucy and her husband Norm are the owners. We would never try to compete with them. Hiro only makes burgers for close friends and family. We will never put them on the menu," Melissa said in a low tone while leaning in close. Then the woman placed her index finger to her lips in the universal sign of secrecy.

Carrie smiled since she and Melissa were the only people inside Phong's Wok, likely because it was just a little after ten in the morning. "Sounds great. I'd like to try one."

"You'll be in for a treat. I'll be right back." Melissa walked into the kitchen.

Carrie looked out the big glass window onto the park. People were scurrying about, getting ready for the big paintball event. It was obvious to her that everyone got involved with the affair. She thought about Ethel O'Leary and her two husbands, Patrick and Sam, whom she'd met right here at the Wok. Ethel was a grand champion of the game and had invited her to join in the festivities.

I wonder if I could take out that eighty-year-old woman. She grinned. *I doubt it, but it would be fun to try.*

Fun? Until coming to Destiny she'd never had much fun. Now, only being in the wonderful town a couple of days, she couldn't seem to stop smiling. She'd been horseback riding with Josh and Jacob not once, but twice. Enjoyed a picnic. A barbeque. And she knew that having lunch with Melissa was going to be a blast, too. *She has such a cute personality.* These were wonderful memories she was making. She could imagine living in Destiny for the rest of her life. She thought back on the few memories she had from her childhood filled with darkness and fear.

Then her mind drifted back to Josh and Jacob. She couldn't stop thinking about them. In time, things might get more serious with them. She was already falling fast. But was that fair to Josh and Jacob to continue dating them without telling them the whole truth about her memory loss?

Melissa returned carrying a white pot and two matching cups. "Jasmine tea, right?"

"Yes. Thank you."

Melissa sat down across from her in the booth and filled their cups.

She took a sip, enjoying the warmth and aroma of the tea. "Delicious."

"I'm glad you like it." Melissa smiled. "You looked deep in thought when I came out of the kitchen. Is everything okay, Carrie?"

"Everything is wonderful. I just need to stop being so negative."

"My motto is to try to take things one day at a time and enjoy every moment we're given. You might want to try it, too."

"You're a wise woman, Melissa Phong. I will try, but my old habits are going to take time to change. I've just never known real happiness like I've found in Destiny. So I'm scared it will all be taken away from me like everything else has been before in my life."

"Sweetie, worry like that will make you an old woman." Melissa smiled, making her feel even more at ease. "You're in Destiny now where we all take care of each other, so you have nothing to fear. My son, Jacob, had so many problems when he arrived in Destiny. But just look at him now. Both my boys are so happy."

"I thought Jacob was your nephew?"

"Biologically speaking, that's correct. But from the heart, he's Hiro's and my son. You know he changed his last name to Phong, but that's all part of his story that he should tell you. Not me."

That explains why he seems to understand me so well. He has a past, too.

Hiro came out from the kitchen carrying their plates. "Two Chinese-American burgers for two beautiful women." He placed them on the table.

The burgers looked and smelled delicious and were surrounded by fries.

"Thank you, Mr. Phong."

"Hiro, please."

She nodded. "Chinese-American burgers with French fries. Quite the international lunch you've made for us."

"Take a bite of the burger, Carrie. I want to see your reaction."

"Hiro, let the girl enjoy her lunch," Melissa said with a wink. "I have no doubt she'll love it."

"It's okay. I can't wait to try it." Carrie took a bite and marveled at the blend of Asian and American flavors. "How did you do that? I love it. It's like nothing I've ever tasted before. You're a master chef, Hiro. I want the recipe."

The man smiled and shook his head. "It's a family secret, Carrie. I'm sorry, but any time you want a burger I would be happy to make one for you. No problem at all."

"Thank you so much." She took another bite. "So good."

"Speaking of my boys…" Hiro said.

Melissa laughed. "We weren't speaking of our boys, honey."

"Oh well, you should've been." Hiro kissed his wife on the cheek. "Since we're not busy, do you two ladies mind if I join you for a few minutes?"

"Absolutely," Carrie said, dipping a fry into the special sauce. "The more the merrier, Hiro."

Hiro sat down. "Now about my boys, Carrie. Don't you find them very good looking?"

"Hiro." Melissa slapped his hand lightly. "Stop."

Carrie giggled.

"Now, honey, it's a fair question," Hiro said. "Besides, Carrie laughed, so I know she doesn't mind."

"Well, yes, Hiro. Josh and Jacob are very attractive."

The man brought his hands together. "I knew it. You like them, too. You're a beautiful woman, so the three of you will go together very well. Just think of the cute babies, Melissa."

Melissa slapped his hand again, this time a little harder. "Oh my God, Hiro. Don't scare the girl off. Give her a chance to know our boys better."

Carrie loved how these two got along together. They were deeply in love and were so cute and playful with each other.

"What more is there to know, Melissa?" Hiro asked. "Josh and Jacob are handsome, kind, smart, and hard workers."

Yes, they are.

Hiro looked her straight in the eyes and smiled. "They would be a catch for anyone, but they like you, Carrie. So what do you say?"

"I do like them, Hiro, but we've only been horseback riding twice."

"Don't forget the barbeque last night that they went to," he said. "And I know they've been working since early this morning on making your date tonight very special."

"I'm sorry, Carrie, for my husband's lack of manners. But as you can see, there's no stopping him. He's always been a hopeless romantic."

"Romance is how I won your heart, angel." He grabbed her hand and brought it up to his lips. "And if the truth be known, I hear wedding bells in the air for our boys and this beautiful girl." He laughed. "You said you wanted my hamburger recipe, Carrie. This is the only way you will get it."

"I'm not sure how to respond to that." She reached across the table and grabbed the dear man's hand and squeezed. "But I promise to take everything you've said under consideration and get back to you later."

"After the date tonight? Melissa and I were engaged after our second date, Carrie, just so you know. And we've been married for thirty-two years."

The door opened and in walked Matt, Sean, and Jena.

"Over here," she said. "Saved by the cavalry, Hiro."

"That's telling this old goat," Melissa said, giving Hiro a kiss. "But I love him just the way he is. I wouldn't change a thing."

"Neither would I," she said as images of their sons flashed in her mind. It was easy to see that Josh and Jacob had all the good qualities of their parents. *Oh my God, I don't have a nice dress for our date tonight.*

"Hamburgers?" Sean said. "Did you get takeout from Lucy's?"

Melissa sent her a knowing wink. "What do you think, Sean? We serve Chinese food here at Phong's. Not burgers."

She was serious about this being a family secret. Carrie felt good that she'd shared it with her.

"But if you're in the mood for a burger," Melissa continued. "Lucy and Norm can deliver here if you'd like."

"No," he said, none the wiser. "I'd rather have Hiro's famous sesame chicken, if that's okay."

"Crispy beef for me, please," Matt said.

"And what about you, Jena?" Melissa asked.

"Orange chicken with brown rice, please."

"Sit down. All of you. I'll bring a couple of orders of crab puffs. I know how much Matt and Sean like them."

Carrie sent a wink to her and Hiro. "Thank you both."

Jena sat down next to her and Matt and Sean sat across from them.

Being very anxious about her date and having no dress, she turned to Jena. "I need an outfit to wear for tonight. Do you know where I can buy one?"

"I sure do. Once we're finished with lunch, you and I are going shopping. Believe it or not, we have a great boutique right here in Destiny called Lisa's Dresses and More."

"Why don't you take Carrie to Riley's Body Decorations, sweetheart," Sean said. "They have dresses, too. And you know how much I love you in them."

"Riley's Body Decorations? That's a funny name for a dress store," Carrie said.

"That's because it's primarily a tattoo parlor," Matt said.

Jena shook her head. "Sean MacCabe, you know they only sell clothes that would be appropriate for Phase Four."

Carrie had seen the club when she'd ridden into town with Josh and Jacob. "Is that a dance club?"

Sean laughed and Matt grinned.

"Let's just leave it at this, Carrie. They do dance there," Jena said. "I can tell you more about it when we have our girl shopping trip, okay?"

"Sure," she said, more than a little curious about Phase Four.

Chapter Thirteen

With his cousin in the passenger seat, Jacob drove his truck next to TBK's company jet at Walden-Jackson County Airport. He killed the engine and turned to Josh. "I'll get the interior set up while you get the plane fueled."

Josh nodded and jumped out of the truck.

Grabbing the flowers and champagne, he walked up to the plane, smiling. He could tell that Josh was just as excited about their date with Carrie tonight as he was.

"Hey guys." Cooper Ross waved and walked over with Brock Grayson from Shannon's Elite's jet, which was parked next to TBK's. Both men dressed a lot like Dylan Strange and the rest of the men on Black's CIA team. Dark suits. Sunglasses. "Where you two headed?"

"We're taking Matt's sister to Red River, New Mexico, for a steak dinner," he told them.

"We just met her today," Brock said. "She's very impressive and quite beautiful. Good for you two."

"What about you, guys?" Josh asked. "Where are you headed?"

"Thanks to your date's list," Cooper said, "we've got leads for a cult leader that's been on the FBI's most wanted for many years."

"Willie Mayfield. We know." Anger welled up inside him for the pain the bastard had brought on Carrie.

Josh nodded. "She told us all about the asshole last night."

"He's the worst kind of criminal. Abusing women and children." Brock took off his sunglasses and brought out the crucifix that was on a chain around his neck. "And stealing from churches."

"I hope you catch him soon," Josh said, the venom in his tone unmistakable.

Brock returned the chain back under his shirt and put his sunglasses back on. "Cooper and I are flying out tonight and will be interviewing for the next few days several members of churches that are on the list that Carrie gave the team."

"And we get to do something I've never gotten to do in my seven years at the Agency," Cooper said with a grin. "We get to return money to its rightful owners. Treat Miss Dixon well tonight, guys. She's one of the good ones in the world, that's for sure."

"We know." Jacob shook the two men's hand and headed into the plane as Josh headed to the hanger to get someone to bring out the tanker truck to the jet.

Jacob began preparing the cabin for Carrie's arrival. He made sure that the champagne was chilled and that the roses were placed on a special-made table for such decorations so they wouldn't turn over. Then he started looking through the songs on his iPad for just the right one. He had brought the cord to plug it into the jet's sound system. He wanted tonight to be something very special for Carrie, something that would keep her smiling. He knew in his heart that he would never forget this evening with her, just like with their horseback date and picnic or the moment she'd stepped out of the car at the barn when they'd first met. Nothing he could do or say would change how he felt about her.

Josh came into the cabin. "Looks nice, Jacob."

"Thanks, but I'm having trouble picking out the right music."

Josh nodded. "Let me see if I can help."

He handed his iPad to him.

"No. No. No." Josh flipped through the list quickly. "How about this?" he asked, holding out the iPad for him to see.

Jacob looked at the screen. "Good job." Wolfe Mayhem was Destiny's local band and their latest CD was of romantic ballads, featuring Kaylyn singing lead. "Kaylyn has a great voice. These songs will be perfect for our date tonight."

"I agree. Jaris and Chance definitely found their match."

"They sure did." He plugged in his iPad to the plane's cord to the sound system. "And you know, Josh, maybe we have, too."

"You might be right. I sure do care for her a lot already."

"Me, too."

Josh nodded. "I thought so. I always thought we'd end up with one of the local women, one that was fully immersed in the lifestyle. I doubt Carrie even has a clue about BDSM."

"I'm sure she doesn't. But in time we can introduce her to it."

"What if she doesn't respond to it like we do, Jacob? What then?"

"Then it won't matter to me. I would choose her over the lifestyle any day."

Josh smiled. "Sounds like you've fallen for her completely already."

"Yeah, I didn't realize it until I answered your question. What about you?"

"Same answer, though I suspect she has a submissive streak. I believe she would enjoy BDSM as much as we do."

"I guess we'll have to wait to find that out. For now, vanilla all the way."

"Especially tonight. We need to win her, Jacob. I don't want to lose her."

"I don't want that either. Still, I sense there's more pain underneath her surface than she's shared with us."

"More than what she told us about Willie?"

"I think so. What it is, I'm not sure. It's only a feeling I get. I could be wrong."

"I've learned to trust your feelings," Josh said. "We just need to wait until she's ready to tell us everything."

"I agree." Jacob placed his hand on Josh's shoulder. In his terrible childhood days, Josh had been one of the bright lights of hope. Same with Aunt Melissa and Uncle Hiro. Deep down he knew that Carrie still needed light to shine into her darkest places. He wanted to be that light for her, that hope, just like Josh had been for him. "We better head back to town to get ready for our date."

* * * *

Carrie looked at her reflection in the mirror. The red dress fit her body perfectly. "What do you think of this one?"

Rylie, the sales associate, smiled. "You look stunning."

Jena said, "That's the one, Carrie."

"What about accessories?" Rylie asked.

Jena had introduced her to Rylie Gold when they'd entered the store. She'd wondered about her having the same name as the store Sean had mentioned earlier, Rylie's Body Decorations. It turned out her father owned the store and had named it after Rylie. Mr. Gold also owned Phase Four. Jena had informed her the place was a BDSM club. She knew about the lifestyle from her years on the run. Most major cities had one or two of that kind of club, but she'd been surprised to learn that Destiny had one. And even more so that Jena, Matt, and Sean were members.

"You're my shopping expert, Rylie," she said. "Lead the way."

"What about these?" Jena handed her a gorgeous pair of silver earrings. "I think these would work great with the dress."

She held them to her ears, glancing at another mirror. "I love them."

"Now we need shoes and a purse." Rylie walked over to a display and brought back a pair of silver stilettos and a matching clutch. "Do you like these, Carrie?"

"I do."

"You said a seven, right?"

"I'm sure we have your size." Rylie went into the boutique's storeroom and came right back carrying a shoebox. "I was right. Here they are."

Carrie tried on the silver shoes. "They fit perfectly. How do they look with the dress?"

"Let's just say if I wasn't married and I was a guy, I would think you were the most beautiful woman in the world," Jena said.

"She's right, Carrie," Rylie said. "You look gorgeous."

"That's good enough for me. I'm ready to check out."

"This is on me and my guys, Carrie," Jena said, pulling out a credit card from her purse. "This is our way of saying welcome home."

"Is this how Destonians treat newcomers?"

"Exactly," Jena said. "And you'll have your chance to pass it on."

"I certainly hope so because you are spoiling me."

Rylie placed all the items in a bag. "Have fun tonight with Josh and Jacob. They're a couple of hunks."

"I will."

"Don't forget to look for me during the first round of paintball, Jena," the young woman said with a broad smile. "My helmet is bright pink. You can't miss me."

"You're going to enter the game?" Jena asked. "When did you decide that?"

"When you took that call from Matt a few minutes ago. Rylie convinced me how much fun it would be. Besides, I plan on dethroning Ethel."

"Good luck with that," Jena said. "Bye, Rylie."

On the way back to the car, they passed Rylie's Body Decorations.

"What a strange store to name after your daughter," she said to Jena.

"There's a lot of strange things in Destiny, but we love one another."

"I'm curious, Jena. Could we go inside and take a look around?"

"Sure. If you have time."

"I do, my date isn't until seven."

They walked into Rylie's.

The woman behind the counter welcomed them in the warm Destiny way.

A young man, who looked to be barely eighteen, was getting a tattoo on his shoulder. The artist was a man with beautiful tats down both his arms.

"This is her first time," Jena told the woman. "I wanted to show her the club clothes."

"Make yourself at home, girls. If you need anything, just let me know."

"The clothes are in the back, Carrie." Jena led her through a doorway.

Her mouth popped open, seeing all the sexy outfits. "Jena, this skirt wouldn't even cover your ass."

"Actually, I have some smaller. And that is the idea." Jena grabbed a leather crop from a shelf. "That, and other things."

Looking around, Carrie felt excited. What would it be like to wear something from here in front of Josh and Jacob? Would it turn them on? Just thinking about it was certainly getting her charged up.

Jena smiled. "It looks like you might have more questions about BDSM now that I've brought you here."

"I do. Would you mind answering my questions while I get ready for my date?"

"I would love to, Carrie. It's a wonderful lifestyle for many people, though it's not for everyone. You might want to know that Josh and Jacob are in the life."

"I'm so glad you told me because that's important to know before I go on the date with them." She held up a leather halter to her chest, and felt her heart start to race. "Could I really wear this?"

"Yes, you could, and you would look great in it. You should buy it and this mini skirt. But I have no doubt that tonight will be vanilla all the way. You're not in the lifestyle…yet." Jena smiled.

"What do you mean by 'vanilla?'"

"Not BDSM. Traditional. If you're interested in learning more I have some books I can share with you. They explain the lifestyle quite well."

"I guess I have some reading to do." She grabbed the halter and miniskirt. "I'm going to get this outfit and try it on."

Jena's eyebrows rose. "For tonight?"

"Oh God, no."

Chapter Fourteen

Josh walked to the front door with Jacob beside him. Like him, his cousin had put on a sports coat and slacks. Quite different from their typical daywear—boots, jeans, shirt, and cowboy hat—and even more different than their Dom gear, leather vests, pants, and boots.

"Do you think I look okay?" Jacob asked.

He grinned. "Other than that face of yours, you look great."

Jacob laughed. "Hey, my mug is prettier than yours will ever be."

"We'll just let Carrie be the judge of that." Both of them smiling, he rang the doorbell.

Matt opened the door. "What are you two grinning about?"

"We were just asking each other if we looked okay for Carrie." He spread his arms wide, hoping to give Matt a better view. "What do you think?"

Jacob spun around. "Pretty snazzy, right?"

Matt shook his head. "You look like a couple of cowboys trying to play dress-up."

Jena appeared next to Matt. "Wow, you two look fantastic. Carrie is going to be impressed."

"That's what we're hoping for," Jacob said.

"Thanks, honey, for spoiling my fun," Matt said. "Actually, you both did clean up nice. But you better be on your best behavior with my sister, understand?"

He knew better than to get on Matt's bad side. "We've got a fun night planned for her."

"She told me about the steak dinner in New Mexico," Jena said. "Sounds wonderful."

"What?" Matt's volume rose. "New Mexico?"

"Sweetheart, don't be a wet blanket," Jena scolded. "You know Josh is an excellent pilot."

"Absolutely no drinking, Josh," Matt said, still operating in overprotective-brother mode.

"Have I ever had a drink when I have flown you? You know me better than that."

Matt grinned. "I know. I'm just giving you a hard time."

"Yes, you are, you big lug," Jena said. "And you also love having you little sister back so you can be the big brother you always wanted to be."

"And you're the one who found Carrie, baby. You're the best wife in the world." Matt kissed her. "Come on in, guys."

"I'll go get Carrie for you." Jena rushed up the stairs.

Matt led him and Jacob to the living room.

Sean shook their hands. "Damn, guys. Looking good."

Jena's mom and Gary came into the room from the kitchen. Kimmie led the way, carrying her dog Happiness.

"You boys look really handsome tonight," Janet said.

"Yeah," Gary said, kissing her on the cheek. "Almost as good as me."

"Here's your date, guys." Jena stood to the side and Carrie walked next to her.

Josh had never seen such a vision of beauty, and for the first time in his life he felt completely tongue-tied. Her long, dark locks fell to her shoulders and her hazel eyes sparkled.

"Aunt Carrie, you look like a princess." Kimmie ran up to her.

Carrie swept the little girl into her arms. "There's only one princess in this house, and that's you, sweetie."

Finding his voice, he said, "You look gorgeous, Carrie."

Jacob nodded. "You can say that again. Absolutely stunning."

Carrie grinned. "And you two look very handsome."

He took her hand. "Shall we go?"

Janet held up her hand. "Wait. I'll be right back."

As she headed back to the kitchen, Gary said, "Don't look at me. That woman has a mind of her own. I have no idea what she has in mind."

Janet returned with a camera. "I could've taken pictures with my cell phone, but this baby takes the best photos."

"But, Mom, we're ready to go," Carrie said, squeezing his hand and looking at Jacob.

"This will only take a second, and we want this for our memories. One day you'll thank me. Now, you three stand together over there by the fireplace. That's it." Janet snapped a few pictures.

"Can I be in a picture, too, Grandma?" Kimmie asked. "Me and Happiness."

"It's up to Carrie and her dates."

Josh smiled, "Carrie, you better get used to this. Families in Destiny are known for going a little overboard for this kind of thing."

"What kind of thing is this?" Carrie giggled. "It kind of feels like I'm going off to high school prom."

"Exactly," Janet said. "You three are all dressed up for a wonderful evening."

After a few shots with Kimmie and Happiness, followed by one that Gary took with the entire family, Carrie said with a smile, "That's all the paparazzi time for now. We've kept Josh and Jacob waiting long enough."

"Escape," Matt said. "Go now."

Sean put his arm around Janet. "If you don't, this one is sure to keep snapping pictures."

After a few more quick good-byes, he and Jacob walked Carrie out the door.

He grabbed her hand. "You really do look beautiful."

Jacob took her other hand. "He's not lying. Every woman in New Mexico is going to be green with envy when you show up."

"Only because I will be on the arms of the two most handsome men when I arrive."

* * * *

Jacob couldn't keep his eyes off of Carrie in that red dress. When they got to the airport, he got out and held the door for her.

"I still can't believe I'm going to fly tonight. Another first for me." She turned to him and Josh. "Honestly, I'm more nervous than I thought I would be."

He put his arm around her shoulder. "Trust me. Josh is one of the best pilots around. He'll keep us all safe."

They escorted her into the plane.

"Oh my God, this is so luxurious." She ran her hand over the back of one of the leather seats. "This is like the ones you see in the movies."

"Wait until you see the cockpit, sweetheart," Josh said. "It's quite impressive."

"I can't wait to tell Kimmie about this," Carrie said, sitting down. "You're making me feel like a princess."

He loved how excited she was about everything. Despite having lived through the horror of losing her parents and being raised by a madman, Carrie filled every space she entered with light. Still, he sensed her struggle, something she kept hidden and locked away from everyone, a secret darkness. *Tonight, I want her to just have fun and forget whatever troubles haunt her.*

"These are for you, sweetheart." He handed her the red roses.

"You two keep surprising me. Thank you." She smelled the flowers.

Josh opened the champagne, filled two glasses, and handed them over. "While you two enjoy this Dom Pérignon, a gift from my employers, I'll do the preflight since I can't have any. But please save me some for when we get back home."

"Before you go, let's have a toast." He filled one of the flutes with bottled water and handed it to Josh. "To you, Carrie, and to our date tonight."

They clinked their glasses together and took a drink.

"Oh my God. This is incredible."

Josh leaned down. "I must have a taste," he said, and gave her a kiss. "Delicious. I won't be long."

After Josh left, he sat down in the seat next to hers. "I have my own champagne, but I think it would taste better from your lips." He stole a kiss, enjoying the sweetness of her mouth.

She grinned. "What an exciting date already. I can't wait until we're in the air."

"Maybe next time I can fly us."

"You are a pilot, too?" Her gorgeous eyes widened.

"I am, but I'm not certified for this fast of a plane. Josh has been helping me to complete my training. Now that I have such a beautiful passenger to please, I have all the motivation I need to finish."

She grinned. "I don't even know if I'll like flying. I really do have the jitters."

"Maybe a little more champagne will help with that."

"Either way, it tastes so good I wouldn't mind another glass." She held out the flute and he filled it.

"We're all set to take off," Josh said, walking into the cabin. "Come here, pretty lady. You're going to be my copilot."

"You've got to be kidding. This is my first time on a plane."

"Of course, I'm kidding. All you have to do is sit there, be beautiful and enjoy the flight."

"Can you hold my hand?" She stood, moving to face his cousin.

Jacob laughed, and stepped next to her. "She's nervous, Josh."

"I can see that." Josh smiled and pulled her in for a hug. "I'll be a little busy, sweetheart, but I know how to keep your mind occupied and off of worry. You're like anyone else, Carrie. The unknown is difficult, but once you get the feel of things you'll do just great. Now, let me show you." Josh led her into the cockpit.

Carrie's eyes were wide. "This looks more like the controls for a spaceship than a plane."

"State of the art," Josh said, helping her get into the copilot's seat and buckling her in.

"I'm going to be right behind you in the navigator's seat. So if you need me, I'm right here," he said, fastening his seat belt.

"That does make me feel better, Jacob. Thanks."

He placed his hand on her shoulder. "Take deep breaths, nice and slow. That's it. You're going to love it I'm sure."

Once they all had their headphones on, Josh turned to Carrie. "Now listen carefully, sweetheart. This is your job."

"I have a job?"

"I want you to keep your eyes on the outside." Josh was clearly giving her a task to keep her mind busy and her worries at bay. Smart guy. "Tell me any landmarks you see. Lakes. Mountains. Roads. Got it?"

"I'll try," she said softly.

Josh grabbed her hand. "You'll do just fine."

When Josh revved the engines for takeoff, Jacob placed both his hands on Carrie's shoulders. "How are you doing?"

"Pretty good."

Josh got on the radio. "Walden-Jackson Ground, Learjet TBK73, at terminal ramp taxi for an IFR departure south to Red River, New Mexico, with information Delta."

The tower gave the clearance for takeoff and Josh taxied to the runway.

He revved the engines, and Carrie gasped and held on tight to the armrest.

"Here we go, sweetheart," Josh said. The jet shot down the runway and in no time at all was aloft.

"Wow." Carrie turned around, smiling. "This is so much fun. I wasn't scared at all."

"Oh really?" Josh said and they both laughed.

Chapter Fifteen

"Copilot to pilot," Carrie said with a grin, playing up the aviation talk.

Josh turned to her and smiled. "Go ahead, copilot."

"There's a large lake on our right up ahead, but so far no sign of the Loch Ness Monster."

He and Jacob laughed. The entire flight had been so fun and they'd teased each other the whole time.

"Good job, Carrie. That's Sanchez Reservoir." Jacob was looking at an aviation map. "We're about to cross into New Mexico. You're really getting good at spotting things."

"She sure is," Josh said, making her feel so proud. "We'll be landing in Red River in about twenty minutes."

"I'm glad," Jacob said from behind her. "I'm starving. Flying sure does build up a person's appetite."

"It must," she said. "I'm hungry, too. But I wouldn't mind flying all evening."

Josh smiled. "So I'll take that to mean you're not afraid to fly any more, sweetheart. Am I right?"

"Yes, you are. I love it. Jacob mentioned that you're helping him with his classes to get certified for this jet."

"I am."

"Would you take on a complete newbie like me to teach? I really want to become a pilot."

"Lucky for you I have my instructor's license," Josh told her. "Of course I would love to teach you. But you've only taken off in a plane. You might want to wait to decide until after we land. Descending is quite different. In fact, we are ready to start our descent now." Josh radioed the Red River tower, and excitement washed over her.

Unlike during takeoff, Josh was slowing the plane's velocity. The ground below didn't rush by so quickly. "I'm not scared at all," she told them both. "This is amazing."

When the wheels of the plane hit the runway, she didn't gasp. Josh was in total control. She felt completely safe, thanks to him. She'd gotten to enjoy the entire trip from the airport near Destiny to here without worrying one bit.

When they walked down the stairs out of the plane, she saw a black stretch limo with a uniformed driver standing next to it.

"A limo?"

Josh bowed in front of her. "Your chariot awaits, my lady."

Jacob put his arm around her shoulder. "It will take us all to the steakhouse."

"I've never been in a limousine before either. I really do feel like a princess tonight."

The scenery out the windows of the limo was stunning. The vehicle had a fully stocked bar, a television set, and incredible comfy seats.

"You like?" Josh said.

"I like it very much," she confessed. "I could get used to this very fast."

Red River, New Mexico, was a small town nestled in a mountain valley. The car stopped in front of the steakhouse, which looked like a giant red barn to Carrie. Then the driver opened the door for them, and they all exited the limo and went inside.

The interior of the steakhouse was rustic and charming, a very clean restaurant with wagon wheels for chandeliers.

The hostess led them to a table by one of the large windows in the front, allowing them full view of the beauty outside.

After finishing the delicious meal, Josh and Jacob took her dancing at a nearby hall. The band played country music and she quickly caught on to the two-step. The guys were good teachers and dancers.

The band took a break, and they left the dance floor for a quiet table. "This whole night has been amazing, but I'm not sure my legs can hold up for more dancing."

"We got breaks, but you didn't." Josh took a sip of his water.

"I didn't want any breaks. I've never enjoyed dancing so much. I really like country music, too."

Jacob gave her a kiss, and she melted into him. "And now that you're a champion at the two-step, we'll be sure to take you as often as you want. I wish we could stay all night, but all three of us have to get back for the big paintball event tomorrow."

"Yes, we do," she said. "I'm going to unseat Ethel as champion."

"If anyone could, sweetheart, it would be you. But trust me, Ethel is quite the competitor. She won't go down without a fight. What time do we need to leave for the airport, Josh?"

"If you two are ready, I think we should go now."

Excited to be back in the air, she jumped to her feet. "I call copilot seat."

They both laughed.

"You got it, Carrie." Josh put his arm around her shoulder and they walked out of the steakhouse.

Sitting between Josh and Jacob inside the limo, she took their hands. "Thank you for such a fantastic evening."

"Our pleasure, sweetheart," Jacob said. "The truth is I've never had this much fun on a date in my whole life."

"Me either," Josh said, stroking her hair.

She looked out the side window. The full moon illuminated the landscape in a cool blue hue. It looked like a place out of a fairy tale.

"This is my first time in New Mexico. I had no idea how beautiful it was."

"Not as beautiful as you," Jacob said, kissing her cheek.

She leaned her head against his shoulder and continued taking in the countryside. The limo passed a small church that looked painfully familiar to Mrs. Kearns's church. Painted white with a tall steeple. A picket fence surrounding the building. An arched double door that led the members inside.

Her mind flashed back to that painful time, and she closed her eyes, trying to will it away. But it wouldn't go.

"Everything okay, Carrie?" Jacob said.

"Yes. I'm just a little tired is all," she answered, not wanting to spoil the good time they'd had together. How could he read her so easily? She didn't know.

As they entered the plane, she still couldn't shake off the memory of Bronte, Texas. Willie had been the one to con those people, not her. And yet she felt responsible in some way. What could she have done? Nothing. She had only been a little girl. But knowing the facts was different than feeling the past.

"I'm going to start the pre-flight. You two relax." Josh left her alone with Jacob.

"Are you thirsty, Carrie?" Jacob opened the little fridge. "There's bottled water. You want one?"

"Yes. Thank you."

He handed her the water and gave her a sweet kiss.

She felt tears well in her eyes.

How can I be so selfish with him and Josh? I'm no good for them. This can't end well. Bad things follow me. They always have. They always will.

"What's wrong, Carrie?"

"Oh Jacob, this is so wonderful. It's just that…I've been running from darkness for a very long time. It's all I've known. And since I came to Destiny, since I found my brother and a whole new family, and since meeting you and Josh…I've never experienced such happiness. I'm just afraid this will all end."

"I promise you everything will be all right."

"How can you know that?" Carrie looked into Jacob's eyes, wanting so much to believe him.

"Because I know darkness, too. It nearly destroyed me." He grabbed her hands, squeezing them, giving her comfort. "When I was a kid my biological mother stayed high. She was a drug addict—cocaine, meth, heroin. Whatever she could get her hands on."

"Oh my God, Jacob. How horrible." Her heart broke for him.

"I don't remember my biological father. He left three months after I was born and never came back. Afterward, my mother went through men just to get money for drugs. When I was seven, I came home from school and found her passed out in the bathroom with a gash on her forehead. I called Aunt Melissa. They're sisters. She and Uncle Hiro came and pulled me out of the squalor and got my mom in rehab."

She realized his life had been hell, too.

"Once my mom was clean, I went back to live with her. But it didn't last. Never. She would relapse and then go back in rehab, time and again. Finally, she married a guy who seemed nice at first and I had big hopes I would finally have the family I'd always wanted. But in a very short time I learned that wasn't going to happen. Her new husband was a mean drunk. One night he was beating my mother and I tried to stop him. That's when he turned his rage on me. I ended up with broken ribs. This continued and I never told anyone, including Aunt Melissa and Uncle Hiro. I was just so scared. The only light in my life was the summers I got to spend in Destiny during the school break. Josh tried to get me to tell him everything, and I almost did, many times. He's like a brother to me."

"More than *like* from what I've seen," she said, her heart breaking at Jacob's tragic story. "You *are* brothers."

"That's true. I trust Josh more than any man I've ever known. We might have had very different childhoods, but he has always understood me better than anyone else. I wasn't always the most pleasant person to be around because my darkness would consume me, but Josh never gave up on me, even when I didn't want to talk to anyone. He would just be there. Never pushing me. Just waiting quietly until I was ready to open up."

She wondered if Josh would understand her darkness as much as he had Jacob's.

"At sixteen, I left and never looked back. My life was so much better, and then my mother was killed and I started having nightmares."

Her eyes welled up with tears. "Who killed your mother?"

"Her bastard husband, the drunk. According to the police report, he had downed a bottle of whiskey and then beat her to death." Jacob's voice lowered and his hands curled into fists. "I kept thinking if I hadn't left I might have saved her. That's what gave me the nightmares."

She felt the tears fall from her eyes. "Jacob, how did you survive?"

"With help." He cupped her chin. "You and I know what pain is, Carrie. Real pain."

She nodded.

"Like me, you had to learn how to live on your own, how to rely on what you could do and no one else. But that isn't really living, is it?"

"No." She looked into his eyes and saw her own reflection in the darkness of his pupils.

"Even living with Aunt Melissa and Uncle Hiro, I still couldn't get over my nightmares. They encouraged me to see Sam O'Leary. You met him at lunch the other day with Ethel and Patrick."

"I remember him."

"He's a psychiatrist. I balked at the idea at first, afraid what a shrink might unearth in the dark reaches of my mind, but I eventually went to him. Sam showed me that there wasn't anything I could've done to save my mother. She was on a path of self-destruction of her own choosing. And the son of a bitch is in prison for the rest of his life. My nightmares are gone. All of them. Carrie, I encourage you to see Sam. I truly believe he can help you, too." Jacob leaned over and pressed his lips tenderly to hers. "Carrie, I'm glad I got all this out because I want you to know how much I trust you."

"And I trust you," she said, leaning into him. Hearing about his childhood had made her feel even closer to him.

"Sweetheart," he said, stroking her hair. "I don't want there to be any secrets between us. I care for you, Carrie. I care for you deeply."

Her heart seized in her chest. "Jacob, there's still more I need to tell you and Josh."

Josh came into the cabin. "Why the serious looks on your faces?"

"I told her about my past," Jacob said. "It was important to me that she knew everything about me. And Carrie says there's something she wants to share with us."

Josh moved to the chair beside her and took her hand. "Carrie, you can tell us anything, no matter what it is. I'm here for you and so is Jacob."

"I believe you." She looked into his eyes, thinking about how he'd helped Jacob out of the pit of darkness. "I need to tell you. I want to tell you. But it is very hard. I've never shared this with anyone before."

Josh nodded and kissed her. Then he leaned back, keeping hold of her hand. He didn't push her, but just sat there waiting, like he'd done with Jacob before.

Waiting for her courage to build, she said, "Maybe Jacob is right. Maybe Sam can help me."

"Are you having nightmares, too, sweetheart?" Jacob asked.

"No. I used to about the fire, though in the bad dream I could only smell smoke. I always woke up screaming."

Jacob put his arm around her. "But no more?"

"No. Not in a long time." She took a deep breath, ready to tell the two men she trusted most in the world her darkest secret. "I'm not sure how to say this. My mind isn't normal. It's broken. I have entire gaps in my past, voids that I cannot get to. The only thing I remembered about Matt was the color of his eyes, and even then I wasn't sure that memory was real."

"You were only three when you last saw him, Carrie," Jacob said. "It's a wonder you remembered anything about him at all."

"It's not just that, Jacob. You both remember that list I kept of all the churches?"

They nodded.

"I remember some of them, but most of the names of the churches I don't recognize even though I'm the one who wrote them down on my list. Crazy, I know. The few memories I do have are not good. Having to put on a smile when all I wanted to do was cry. Willie beating me, over and over, until I passed out. He is the only constant memory I have. He and Mrs. Kearns."

"The woman who taught you about horses and the stars," Josh said.

"I think she really cared for me. I had even planned on telling her all about what Willie had done, but before I could we were gone. And so was my chance to escape. Guys, I don't know why my memories disappear, but they do. What happens if I forget you, forget all we've shared together?" She leaned back in her chair, hating what she must say next. "You two deserve a woman who is sane, a woman without so much baggage…a woman who is not a mental case like me." She closed her eyes, feeling her heart begin to rip apart. *I can't ask them to stay. It wouldn't be fair.*

Josh wrapped his arms around her. "Look at me."

She opened her eyes and gazed into his.

"You are not a mental case."

"But—"

"No buts." Josh's tone was firm and commanding, reaching something deep inside her, a part of her that wanted to be cared for, to be protected, to be conquered so she could surrender all her fears.

Jacob touched her cheek. "I'm certainly no expert, but I've read that when people have gaps in their memory, it's often just a defense mechanism. A way to survive and get through very dark times. I'm certain Sam could help you with this."

"Listen to him, sweetheart. It makes sense what he's saying. Jacob has been through hell and back," Josh said. "So have you. You had such a horrible childhood with no one to turn to. But now you do. You have us."

Josh and Jacob were the heroes she'd been searching for her whole life, two knights to rescue her from Willie, from the nightmares of dark smoke, from the horrors that had taken away her memories.

Josh kissed her, filling her with hope. "We won't leave you. We won't let you down."

Jacob squeezed her hands, and the darkness fled. "Whatever you need, we're here."

Chapter Sixteen

Josh saw the light return to Carrie's hazel eyes.

She got up on her tiptoes and offered him a kiss. He leaned down and devoured her mouth, tracing her lush lips with his tongue. He deepened their kiss and pulled her soft body in close.

He'd thought it best to go slow with her, to give dating a try. Dating? That wasn't something he and Jacob had ever done with any woman. Not in the traditional way at least. But they'd both known Carrie deserved their best effort. And she was so much more than even they'd imagined. The pain and suffering she'd survived would've sent most into an asylum, or worse to suicide. But she'd survived a desperate past. The only scars left were the memories she'd lost. She was strong, but she saw herself as broken.

When he released her lips, he saw her cheeks turning a deep pink. When she smiled he knew her dark mood had vanished. "I want you, Carrie."

Jacob kissed the back of her neck. "I want you, too."

"And that's what I want." Her admission of desire took hold of him and his insides began to burn. "I need both of you."

"God, you're so perfect." He kissed her again. "It's us who needs you." Every dominant part of him wanted to rip her clothes off and demand her sweet submission. But she wasn't in the life. She hadn't been trained. They hadn't even discussed BDSM with her. He turned to Jacob. "Vanilla, right?"

Jacob nodded. But it was obvious he was struggling to keep his Dom side at bay.

"Vanilla?" Her smile alone thrilled him to no end. Whatever it took to make sure she was happy he would do. "Guys, I know what you mean when you say 'vanilla.' Traditional sex."

He was shocked to hear her words. "Who told you about 'vanilla' sex?"

"Jena. She gave me a book about BDSM. I only had time to read a few chapters before our date, but I did learn a lot." She grinned. "Jena also told me you two are resident Doms at Phase Four, the BDSM club in Destiny."

"Oh she did, did she?" Jacob used his Dom tone.

She giggled. "Yes, Masters. She did."

By the look on Jacob's face, he was clearly just as happy as Josh was at her excitement.

"We are Doms, sweetheart," he told her, also using his most commanding voice.

It clearly had an impact on Carrie, as she looked down at her feet and continued smiling. She was delightfully nervous, and that pleased him very much.

He cupped her chin. "Look at us."

She instantly obeyed, and Josh felt his cock and balls stir in his jeans. He so wanted to play with her at the club, teach her all about the life, help her to see how amazing and wonderful she really was, not broken at all. But he was glad their first play was here, on the plane, where he felt in control more than anywhere else. He was captain and Jacob was co-captain. She was their passenger, and tonight they would take her on a most intimate flight.

"So, little sub, you've read a few chapters in a book," Jacob said. "We made love to you at our picnic, taking little tastes of your sweetness, discovering what you respond to, what turned you on, so we could give you pleasure. BDSM goes beyond anything you've ever done before. You want to take this ride?"

"Yes, Sir. I want to learn everything."

"Everything?" Jacob turned to him. "Damn, she's killing me, and we haven't even started."

His cock pulsed and stretched at her admission. "Jacob, is she pure heaven or what?"

Jacob kissed her deeply, like a man dying of thirst. "She's everything I've ever dreamed of, Josh. An angel."

"*Our* angel." He gazed into her gorgeous hazel eyes.

"Guys…I mean Masters…I'm a bit nervous, even more than I was about flying, but I'm also excited."

"BDSM is all about pleasing you, sweetheart. A Dom's ultimate satisfaction only comes when his sub is able to trust him completely to guide her into a state of blissful release. What did that book tell you about safe words?"

She recounted what she'd learned, which fit his and Jacob's protocols perfectly.

"Very good, little sub," Jacob said, kissing her neck. "What words shall we choose?"

"How about 'flight' for when I'm wanting more, and 'descend' for when I want you to slow down, Masters?"

"You really do love flying now, don't you?" Josh reached under her dress and pulled her panties to her ankles. "What word would you say for us to stop?"

"Does 'crash' seem like a good safe word, Masters?"

"Perfect, sweetheart," Josh said. "Fasten your seatbelt. Master Jacob and I are going to take you on a long flight."

* * * *

Carrie trembled excitedly, anticipating her first lesson in BDSM. When Josh had removed her panties, she realized she was in for the ride of her life.

"Remove your dress, sub," Josh commanded, taking off his shirt.

Jacob was also undressing.

Wanting to please them, she immediately took her dress off.

"Step out of your panties and remove your bra."

When she was standing completely naked in front of them, Jacob said. "Now, spin around for us, little sub. I want to get a good look at you."

She felt damp just from parading in front of them. It was so titillating. *I'm so turned on.*

"Did you not hear me?" Jacob asked, his tone deepening. "Spin around."

"Yes, Master. I'm sorry." She twirled in front of them.

"Absolutely gorgeous." Josh's gaze moved up and down her body, and so did Jacob's.

It was obvious they wanted her. They'd said so with words and with lusty stares.

They'd taken off all their clothes except their pants. They didn't seem in a hurry to remove them.

Why? Is that part of the lifestyle, too? Or are they simply trying to tease me?

This was her first lesson in BDSM. They were in charge. They were Doms. She was a sub. She only had to listen and obey. That was her role according to the chapters she'd read in Jena's book. Simple. Easy. No wondering what to do next, only to feel. *God, who knew I would love this so much?* She wanted to learn everything she could from them—from her two Doms.

Are they ever going to touch me? As if they were reading her mind, they began caressing her. Their touches felt so good on her skin.

Josh stood behind her, kissing her neck and massaging her breasts. Standing in front of her, Jacob ran his hands down her sides and pressed his lips to hers. She could feel her temperature rising.

"Pain leads to pleasure." Josh pinched her nipples, delivering a sweet sting. "Pain is a key, a tool. When a Dom delivers just the right amount, subs, like you, can let go and tune completely into their bodies. It focuses the mind, pushing away all the worries of the outside world." He rolled her nipples between his fingers, and she felt them throbbing, creating a line of electricity that shot up and down her body, settling between her thighs. "Let us open the door for you, Carrie. A door to a place you will never forget and from deep within yourself you will long to return to often. We want you to experience what's behind that door. Do you want to know what it is, sweetheart? What's behind that door?"

"Yes, Master," she whispered, tingling like mad with desire. "Please tell me."

"It's a state of complete and utter bliss," Josh said. "Turn around and face me."

She spun around and hated seeing him still partially clothed, though she could see his cock bulging underneath the fabric of his pants. She glanced over at Jacob and saw the same thing. She smiled, glad that their bodies couldn't lie to her. Josh and Jacob wanted her, wanted her in the worst way. "When are you two going to take off those damn slacks?"

Josh grinned wickedly and Jacob laughed.

"What did you say to us, sub?" Josh asked firmly.

"When are you going to take off those damn slacks…,Masters?"

"Shall I go first?" Josh asked Jacob.

Go first? I guess Josh is going to take his pants off first. She grinned.

"Rock, paper, scissors?" Jacob said.

"Why do either of you have to go first?" she asked. "Just take off your slacks at the same time."

They both laughed.

"We're not taking off our pants yet, little sub," Jacob said.

Confused, she asked, "You're not?"

"You sure do have a lot to learn. No, we're not, but we are deciding who gets to spank you first."

"Spank me? Why? What did I do?"

"It's obvious that you only read a few chapters of Jena's book," Josh said. "Trust me, Carrie, you can't learn everything about the life just in books. We're going to spank you because you were trying to take charge."

"I was?"

He grinned and nodded. "You want us naked, out of our pants. You told us so. You even cursed. 'Damn pants.'"

"Oh God, I did. I didn't mean to, Masters." She felt heat rush to her face.

Jacob kissed her on the cheek. "I'm sure you didn't, but we're going to teach you to remember who is in charge."

He and Josh did a single round of the rock, paper, scissors game. She smiled, seeing a glimpse of the boys they'd been before, brothers who cared deeply for each other. Josh had been a steady light in Jacob's horrible past. With Josh's help, Jacob had made it through the darkness.

"Paper covers rock," Josh said. "I go first. Come here, sub. Bend over my lap."

Trembling, she draped her body over his legs. Submitting to them seemed as natural as breathing to her. But how could that be? Her whole life she'd had to be guarded. Oh, she could be pleasant, friendly, and warm on the outside. But the inside? That was what had to be kept safe and hidden. From everyone. But now? With her two gorgeous beasts? She couldn't hold back anything. This was intimacy on a level she'd never known existed.

"Remember what I said, sweetheart, about the key to bliss. Trust me, and you will discover how much pain and pleasure go hand in hand."

"I do trust you, Master. I trust you both so very much." The truth. Saying it aloud sealed it in her heart like a brand that would never go away.

Josh caressed her bottom, making her even warmer. When he slapped her ass, she gasped. He landed slap after slap to her ass. None of them really hurt. They only just stung. And the little bites to her flesh from him turned her on and raised her pressure.

Josh sent his hand between her legs and threaded his fingers through her pussy. "She's wet, Jacob, and ready for your discipline."

Josh lifted her up and stood.

Jacob took his place in the seat, and Josh lowered her down onto his lap, still face down.

"I'm going to spank you five times," Jacob said. "I want you to count them aloud after each one, sub."

"Yes, Master."

His first slap took her breath away, biting into her ass just a little more than Josh's had. She bit her lower lip and closed her eyes. What were these strange feelings rolling through her mind? She thought about sitting up, telling them she'd changed her mind, that this wasn't really what she wanted. But that would be a lie. She'd run for so long. So very long. Could she stay? Stay with them? Her heart pounded even harder, and she remained across his lap, waiting.

Jacob massaged her ass gently, and she could feel the hardness of his cock pressing through his pants against her abdomen. "Little sub?"

"Oh yes," she said breathlessly. "One, Master. That was one slap."

He swung his hand down again, and the sting multiplied on top of the others, building an unexpected rush of crushing need inside her.

"Two, Master." *What is this? Why is my body responding like this?*

Jacob fingered her pussy softly. "Very good, angel. You're doing great."

His words of praise only added to her suffering. He and Josh had promised her a ride that she would never forget, and damn they were delivering.

Another slap to her ass sent her reeling. Her mind was fuzzy as the needs of her body took her over completely. "Three, Master."

Again, Jacob massaged her ass and pussy. Pain, followed by pleasure. They seemed completely intertwined to her.

Another slap, this one harder than any that had come before, followed by his sweet touch, making her feel like she was floating on air. "Four, Master."

The final slap landed in the center of her ass, and her desire for them to be inside her heightened and spread throughout her body. Her clit began to throb from his touches and her pussy got even wetter.

"Five, Master. Five," she panted out the last number.

Jacob kissed her bottom. "You did so good, little sub."

"What state are you in, sweetheart?" Josh asked, stroking her hair.

"Good, Master. I'm in a very good state." Recalling the safe words they'd agreed on, she added. "Flight. I want to fly more, Sir."

Just as Josh had done moments ago, Jacob lifted her off the chair, keeping her in his arms as he stood. "You said you wanted us out of our pants." He lowered her down and then moved next to Josh. Her two Doms stood in front of her, looking like sexy Greek gods.

"You have to take them off, understand?"

"Yes, Master. I can finally get rid of the damn pants?" she asked as innocently as she could.

They laughed.

"Yes, baby," Jacob said. "You can get rid of our damn pants."

She removed his pants first and then Josh's.

"On your knees," Josh ordered.

"Yes, Sir," she said, taking a long look at both their hard cocks.

She reached out, wrapping one hand around each of them.

They both groaned as desire slid out over her skin. She tightened her grasp, smiling as they each closed their eyes.

They'd given her so much. The horseback ride and picnic together, where they'd shown her such joy and pleasure. Coming to the barbeque to celebrate with her family. This incredible date, making her feel like the center of the world, a princess. *Their princess.* The last few days had been a whirlwind, and she loved every breathless second.

She inhaled deeply, taking in their scent. Clean masculinity with a hint of spiciness. They smelled so incredible. "I want to taste you, Masters."

Josh tugged on her hair lightly. "Show us what that gorgeous mouth of yours can do, sweetheart."

Jacob touched her cheek and smiled. "Do it now, angel, or I'll have to bend you over my knee again." He grinned, and more tingles erupted inside her.

She kissed the tip of his cock and then Josh's. She licked her lips, tasting their little salty pearl drops. She was thirsty for more, much more. She licked around the head of Josh's cock, discovering its contours, slipping her tongue into his tiny slit.

"That feels so good." He gave a light tug on her hair.

She pumped on Jacob's cock as she swallowed the head of Josh's, swirling her tongue. They both groaned deeply, and that spurred her on more.

Needing to taste Jacob, too, she switched, pumping on Josh's cock while sucking in the head of Jacob's.

Jacob blew out a hot, lusty breath. "I love the feel of your mouth around my cock, angel. You're driving me crazy. Suck harder. Take more."

Without hesitation and wanting so much to please both of them, she swallowed as much of him as she could take of his long thickness.

He groaned, thrusting deep. "God, that feels so good. I need you, Carrie."

His words swept over her.

I need you, too. I need both of you. Back and forth. She sucked and pumped on them until she could sense they were both getting close.

"Get up," Jacob commanded in a tone that demanded her instant obedience. "I don't want to come yet."

He and Josh helped her to stand. She looked up at them, taking in their naked, beautiful forms. Their cocks, still wet from her mouth, pulsed with arousal.

She held her breath as Josh got a condom out of his pants pocket. He ripped the package open and slid the condom down his shaft. His hungry stare never left her.

Jacob moved behind her, and drew her in close. Her back nestled into his chest and Josh pressed his muscled body into her front. *This is where I belong. Between them.* Here she felt safe, sheltered. Nothing could hurt her as long as she was in their arms.

Josh kissed her lips and Jacob the back of her neck. She could feel their erections pressing against her body, Josh's on her abdomen and Jacob's on her ass. She wrapped one arm around Josh. With the other, she reached back until her fingers touched Jacob.

Josh bent down and swallowed her nipple, tracing little circles around the tip. Jacob kissed his way down her back to her ass. He parted her cheeks with his hand and tongued her anus. Her body responded to their intimate caresses and the pressure intensified.

"Have you had anal sex before, little sub?" Jacob's question ignited more shivers inside her, and she felt herself get even wetter.

"No, Master." She'd never even considered it before, knowing such an act would make her too vulnerable. But now, with them, she embraced her vulnerability.

"Don't worry, angel, I know what to do. Everything will be okay." Jacob kissed her ass tenderly. "You can't imagine how pleased I am that you haven't."

Josh stepped back and opened his satchel. He brought out a tube of lubricant and handed it to Jacob. He smiled and then kissed her deeply.

Josh and Jacob were in control. With them, like this, she didn't have to look over her shoulder wondering what monster might spring from the shadows. With them, she was protected and cherished. With them, she could just feel. No worries. Only pleasure.

Jacob once again parted the cheeks of her ass and began applying lubricant to her anus. He circled the tight ring, delivering a generous amount of the slick liquid.

Josh knelt down in front of her. "God, your pussy is beautiful."

She'd never thought of it that way.

Josh's fingers threaded through her wet flesh slowly, until they found her throbbing clit. She moaned, relishing the dual fingering her body was receiving from them.

Jacob sent a finger past her tight ring, and she felt herself clench. "Breathe, angel. Just breathe."

"Yes, Master," she panted out.

"That's it. Let me in." His words came out ragged and full of heat.

"You're getting to her," Josh said, dragging his tongue over her pussy while continuing to press on her clit. "She's giving me her sweet cream."

"Tell me what you're feeling, sub," Jacob ordered, sending another thick digit into her ass.

"Yes, Master. I'm...feels good." She squirmed as he thrust his two fingers in and out of her anus. "Like nothing I've ever felt before. So...tight." She closed her eyes, wondering how she would ever be able to take his cock back there.

"You're holding your breath," Josh said. "Breathe, sweetheart."

As Jacob continued pushing in and out of her ass with his fingers, she obeyed, though her inhalations were shallow. Powerful need to have them claim her inside and out shook her entire body.

Jacob stood and pressed the head of his cock to her anus, causing her to whimper just a little. He kissed the back of her neck. "Relax, angel. It might feel a little strange and uncomfortable at first, but trust me, we're going to give you so much pleasure you won't think it's possible. But it is. With me and Josh."

She felt her eyes water, bracing herself for him to thrust into her ass. How could she take him this way? She wasn't sure, but trusted him with every part of her, including her backside.

"Take a deep breath and hold it for me, Carrie." Jacob held her by the sides.

Josh used his tongue to press on her clit.

"That's it, angel. Now let it out nice and slow."

"Yes, Master." She emptied her lungs all the way and then she felt Jacob thrust into her, past the tight ring of her anus.

She gasped, feeling pulsations burn inside her. He stretched her out beyond what she'd ever thought possible.

"Keep breathing."

Jacob's words floated through the warm haziness that had taken her over completely. Her ass tightened around his shaft and then released. Again and again. Tight. Release. Electricity ignited along lines that spanned her body. Her clit throbbed and her pussy clenched.

Josh stood and grabbed her. She wrapped her arms around his neck, feeling her eyes water from the hot passion coursing through her. He pulled her legs off the floor and around his waist, thrusting his cock into her pussy.

More sensations flooded her, igniting nerve endings and pleasure spots in her body. She trusted Josh and Jacob with this, with everything—with her very life. "Oh God. Yes. Yes."

Josh's face was tight with desire, and yet his tone was gentle. "Carrie, I love you. I love you so much."

Tears streamed down her cheeks as he continued thrusting in and out of her.

Jacob matched Josh's rhythm perfectly. In and out. "I love you. I want you not just for tonight. I want you forever."

"We both want you forever," Josh added.

Their words melted her utterly.

She loved them. There was no denying it any longer. She'd never known love before. But now she did, inside and out. Josh and Jacob knew how broken she was and still they wanted her in their lives. They wanted something permanent.

"I love you both so much. I want to be yours forever, too."

They both uttered noises that sounded primal, like growls. Their thrusts into her pussy and ass intensified, going deeper, stretching her to the max. She felt every stroke that brought new sensations and multiplied her need beyond the bearable.

They surrounded her, naked skin to naked skin, their cocks rubbing deep inside, their hot breath hitting the skin on her neck and face. The intimacy wasn't just physical in this incredible moment, it was so much more. They were three heartbeats melded together. With them she felt beautiful, powerful, and so very feminine.

"I'm close," she confessed.

"Come for us, angel," Jacob commanded. "Come now." He drove into her ass again and again, as Josh did the same in her pussy.

And then the pressure exploded, releasing overpowering pleasure that flooded every cell in her body. Shivering sensations raced through her, igniting inside her core and shooting down her legs and arms. She was ablaze and more alive than she'd ever been before.

She clenched down on their cocks inside her body with her pussy and ass.

Josh shuddered, and she felt his cock pulse as he came inside her. Jacob groaned and thrust his dick all the way into her ass, releasing his seed.

They held her between them for several delicious moments. Once again, they'd given her shivers, something she'd never felt before with sex. Only with them.

Josh kissed her tenderly. "I love you, Carrie."

"I love you, too."

He and Jacob lowered her back into her seat.

Jacob bent down and pressed his lips to hers. "I love you so much, angel. I can't believe we're so lucky to have finally found you."

Chapter Seventeen

"Hello, Cindy." Holding his cell to his ear, Willie looked at the hundreds of people lining up to register for paintball. There were more players arriving every hour. Sign-up would continue another two hours, all the way up until midnight. The streets around the square were all blocked off. Tomorrow morning the big event would get started.

"Why haven't you taken care of that matter we agreed upon yet?" Trollinger's angry tone came through the phone loud and clear.

"Don't worry about Jaris Simmons, Cindy. It will be my pleasure to eliminate him. In fact, I plan on putting a bullet in the bastard's head tonight. Starting at midnight, Simmons will be working the overnight shift for the event's security, an excellent time to find him alone since nothing gets underway until eight in the morning."

"Perfect. Just let me know when the job is done."

"Did you get the number for me?"

"I did." Trollinger's voice softened. She told him Carrie's cell number. "She's had the same phone for over three years. It wasn't hard to find, Willie."

"You're the tech expert, Cindy. I'm better on the front lines. I think we'll make a good team going forward."

"You think so? Just get the job done and we'll discuss it."

"And you'll have my payment with you when we meet, right?"

"Yes."

The line went dead, and he continued scanning the area. His plans were flawless. Simmons would be easy. So would the plan with Carrie.

He slowly worked his way behind a group of twenty players to keep from being noticed. There was plenty of security, though it seemed they were there primarily to answer questions and keep players away for the non-paintball places in the town. There weren't many inside the city limits, only the residential streets were out of bounds. There wasn't a car allowed on the streets. His rental was parked next to the bridge in the big parking lot with all the other out-of-towners' cars.

The mood that permeated everyone he'd seen was upbeat and full of anticipation for tomorrow, both local and outsider alike. *Idiots. If they want fun, they should use the real thing.* He reached into his jacket to touch his gun. He recalled how thrilling it had been when he took his first life with his own hands. He'd felt invincible and full of power. What a rush. Three heartbeats had been silenced by his bullets. Crimes that would go unsolved forever. Just like the fire in Belco. Those fools' lives had ended because of him. The authorities had known he'd escaped, but they still hadn't been able to find him. They never would.

Simmons walked right in front of him with a blonde woman on his arm and a black guy who had a German shepherd on a lead. It was obvious the black guy was blind. He'd already learned that these three were married. *Sickening.*

He smiled at them as they passed. *Enjoy yourself, Simmons. These will be your last hours among the living.*

The trio turned left by one of the statues in the park. He kept moving forward. Everyone he passed had broad smiles on their sick faces. *It will be so much fun to bring this town to its knees.*

Cindy Trollinger and her brother had been at war with Destiny for quite a while, losing almost every battle. Hell, her brother had even lost his life. *Perhaps Cindy needs my talents more than she realizes.* He had finesse and charm that could be used to ease the minds of the unsuspecting. She had a huge bank account at her disposal and excellent contacts to call on when needed. Together, they would be unstoppable.

Destiny wasn't different from any other town he'd bested, except their strange practice of poly relationships. Disgusting in every way to him. Why marry the bitches? He would fuck as many as he wanted. Always had. But marriage? That was between one man and one woman. And Carrie was meant to be his.

He didn't give a damn how the assholes around here lived. He wouldn't be here long enough to care. Still, he had no doubt that the citizens of Destiny were just as gullible as anyone else he'd ever conned.

Like taking candy from a baby.

* * * *

Jacob walked Carrie to the door of her family's home. Josh was on the other side of her, holding her hand.

"Guys, tonight was the most fantastic night of my life. I love you both so very much."

"I love you, sweetheart." Josh kissed her. "Expect more nights like this in your future."

"Many more," Jacob said, pressing his mouth to Carrie's soft lips. "I love you, angel."

She smiled and hugged them both. "I better get some sleep. Tomorrow is a big day."

"And if you're going to unseat Ethel as champion, you'll need all the rest you can get," he said.

"She's really that good?"

"Let's just say I'm glad I'm working security this year," Josh said. "Last year, Ethel took me out within fifteen minutes of every game round."

"I only lasted ten minutes," he confessed. "But I'm not sure she's expecting someone as strong as you to show up on the field. My money is on you to win this year.

Carrie smiled. "It better be." She grabbed the handle but didn't turn it. "I plan on reading more of Jena's book before I go to sleep."

Josh grinned wickedly. "If you want more lessons, we can—"

"Josh, she needs her rest." He smiled and touched her cheek. "We will show you more about the life as soon as we can. Tomorrow is a big day for all of us, but especially you."

"You will take me to Phase Four sometime?"

"When we think you're ready, yes."

She got up on her tiptoes and kissed him lightly on the mouth. Then she turned to Josh and did the same.

"Good-night." She opened the door and went inside.

When the door closed, he looked at Josh. "We found the woman of our dreams."

"Yes, we have. She's the one."

"No doubt about it." He thought about how great it had been on the plane, making love to her again. She'd responded without reservation to the spankings he and Josh had given her. At her sexual core, she was a submissive.

As they walked back to the truck, he still couldn't quite believe how wonderful his life had become. Carrie was his and Josh's future. She made him look forward to settling down and starting a family.

Once in the truck, his cell rang. "Hi, Aunt Melissa."

"Jacob, is Josh with you?"

"Yes."

"Good. Would you boys mind going to the sheriff's office and reporting for security duty for the midnight shift? Jaris and Chance were assigned to that shift, but Sugar is delivering her puppies right now. Jaris and Chance need to be there with Kaylyn for Sugar."

"Yes, they do." Sugar was Jaris's black German shepherd and had been by his side during his temporary blindness. Chance, who had been blind since birth, had helped Jaris through the roughest parts of it. The two men had married Kaylyn, who was the singer for Wolfe Mayhem and the owner of the kennel that trained service dogs where Sugar had come from. "We'll take Jaris's and Chance's shifts, Aunt Melissa. No problem at all."

* * * *

Holding the helmet in her hand, Carrie stepped into the kitchen. Jena, Matt, and Sean were sitting at the table. Janet was at the stove, cooking breakfast. "Something smells really good."

"And someone looks good, too," Jena said. "I knew my paintball gear would fit you."

She grinned, donning the helmet. "I feel like a soldier in these camos."

"That's the whole idea," Sean said. "By the looks of you I can see that Ethel O'Leary is in for trouble."

"You're just saying that. I've never played paintball in my life."

Matt laughed. "Sounds like you're getting game-day jitters. You shouldn't been bragging so much, sis. Everyone is expecting you to kick butt."

She took off the helmet and sat down. "What have I gotten myself into?"

"You'll have fun no matter what," Janet said, placing a plate in front of her. "Two eggs over medium. Two slices of buttered toast. Crisp bacon. And a bowl of fruit for our family's only competitor this year."

"She'll make us proud," Matt said. "I have no doubt."

He and Sean would be working as security. Jena had volunteered to man the information booth with some of the other local women.

"What about you, Janet?" Carrie took a bite of the bacon, which was cooked perfectly. "It's not too late to put your name on the list of players."

Janet poured her a cup of coffee. "I'm going to stay here with Kimmie and we're going to be baking all day for the closing ceremonies."

"Where is Kimmie?" she asked, taking a sip from her cup.

"Still in bed," Jena said. "We let her stay up and watch that kid's movie about the rabbit family."

"She sure was excited about seeing it," Carrie said. "I peeked in on her a little before midnight when I got home last night. She and Happiness were asleep."

"We'd just put her to bed. I have no idea how our little girl was able to stay awake for the whole movie," Matt said. "Which reminds me, Carrie, how did your date go with Josh and Jacob?"

"It was incredible. My first time on a plane and first time in New Mexico." She smiled, looking around the table. Jena, Matt, Sean, and Janet cared for her. They were her family. She wanted them to know how happy she was. "And it was the first time for Josh and Jacob to tell me they love me."

She could tell by the looks on their faces they were shocked and excited by her news.

Janet grabbed her hand and squeezed. "And what did you say to them?"

Bursting with joy, she blurted out, "That I love them. That I love them both very much."

"This requires a toast," Sean said, grinning broadly and holding up his cup.

She and the rest lifted their coffee cups.

"To our dear Carrie," he said. "May you have continued happiness with Josh and Jacob in Destiny."

"Here. Here." Jena clinked her cup to hers.

Matt smiled. "Sis, Josh and Jacob are great guys. I know they will make you very happy."

Janet wiped her eyes. "I bet I'll be making a wedding cake very soon for the three of you."

Carrie grinned and squeezed the sweet woman's hand back. "We've only just told each other how we felt. Thinking about a wedding now seems a little too soon, don't you think?"

"Not in Destiny," Jena said. "Once those three wonderful words are uttered it's no time before the bride is walking down the aisle."

Sean nodded and then turned to Janet. "Except when it comes to you and Gary. When can we expect you two to finally tie the knot?"

"Sean's right, Mom," Matt said. "It's long overdue."

"Are you that anxious to get rid of me?" Janet asked.

"No, we figured Gary would just move in," Sean said. "This is a big house. The more the merrier in our book."

"Are you serious?"

"Yes, Mom," Jena said. "We're very serious. We only want you to be happy. You and Gary."

"Knowing that makes me feel so good. Thank you. Gary is in Denver for business. Once he's back I will share with him what you told me." Janet stood, a happy tear streaming down her smiling face. "It's just as much as I love Gary, I've never been happier than I have been living here with all of you. I know Gary is lonely and loves this family, too. He's crazy about Kimmie as much as I am. You've just made me so happy, and I'm sure Gary will be, too." She looked out the window, and Carrie caught a glimpse of her wiping her eyes. "I better get these dishes cleaned up. There's a lot to do today."

Carrie stood. "I'll help you."

Sean glanced back at her and smiled. He'd deflected the conversation for her, for which she was grateful.

"No you won't, young lady," Janet said firmly. "You have a battle ahead of you, and these three have jobs to do. It's already seven-thirty. Go and have fun. I'll clean up the kitchen."

"Okay, Mom." Matt kissed Janet on the cheek.

Sean did the same.

"Thanks for taking care of Kimmie for us," Jena said. "Call me if you need anything."

"We'll be fine, but that reminds me of something." Janet pulled out a note from her apron pocket. "It's for you, Carrie. Kimmie made me promise to give it to you before you left for paintball today."

Carrie smiled, taking the paper from Janet. "I have the best niece in the world, that's for sure."

Kimmie's message touched her heart. It was a picture she'd drawn in bright colors. An arrow pointed to the tallest person in the drawing with the misspelled words "Ant Cary." Above the little girl was the word "me." And at their feet was a white dog, also with an arrow and the word "happynest."

She held it up for the others to see. "We've got an artist in the family. I love this so much. I want to get a frame for it."

"I have one I think you'll like," Janet said. "When you come back I'll show it to you. Now scoot or you'll be late. And good luck."

Chapter Eighteen

Carrie crouched down behind one of the large trees by the Blue Dragon statue, which she'd learned the locals called the Mother Dragon. It was thirty-six minutes into the second round of paintball, and thankfully unlike the first, she hadn't been shot yet. The first round she'd been taken out by an eighteen-year-old sharpshooter seconds after the starting bell. The kid had laughed. It was all in good fun, but she'd stuck her tongue out at him, swearing to find him in the next round.

"I doubt that," he said. "You're a newbie. This is my third year."

Ethel had appeared out of nowhere and shot him. "On the ground, young man. That was a clean shot. And I was champion my first year." The sweet woman came up to her and looked down. "Never underestimate newbies, right Carrie?"

"Right."

"See you in the next round." Ethel had darted off, hiding behind a large tree. She had the sun behind her, which blinded the other gamers. She took them off one by one. Before long, she was the last one standing. No wonder she was the player to beat. She was not only a good shot but very clever, too.

This is so much fun, even though that shot stung. Janet had insisted she wear extra clothing under the camos, and now she knew why.

She spotted a group of three headed her way. She rose up and took them out one after the other. Per the rules, two of them fell to the ground immediately. The last one cursed and remained standing.

"Get down, John," one of his buddies said. "You don't want one of the security guys to kick you out for the rest of the event. We'll do better next round."

John grumbled but finally did stretch out on the ground.

With those three out, she estimated there were only eight more players left, including her and Ethel. *Game on.* Where was the eighty-year-old champion hiding?

She glanced up and down East Street. No sign of anyone. Deciding it was best to remain in the park with all the trees to give her cover, she made her way to the Red Dragon statue on the northeast corner of the park. Remaining low, she moved behind one of the many park benches. Two guys were slinking off to her left. Before she could get off a shot, Ethel jumped out from behind a bush just twenty feet in front of her and shot them both. But the woman hadn't spotted her. The sun was behind her, shielding her from Ethel's view.

Carrie raised her weapon. She had a perfect shot. She tightened her finger on the trigger, but then she saw Ethel smile. How could she shoot her? She couldn't. She lowered her gun and crawled back the way she'd come.

Second place will be just fine for this newbie.

And then she felt the sting in her back. *Damn. She shot me.* She grinned.

Ethel came over to her. "Carrie, a word of advice. This isn't a sentimental game. All is fair in love and war. You should've taken me out when you had the chance."

She laughed. "I'm coming for you next round, Ethel O'Leary. You'll see."

"I have no doubt about that. You're an incredible player, young lady. I still want to win my trophy, so I will be keeping an eye on you." Ethel grinned and then was gone.

On her back staring up into Destiny's clear sky, Carrie thought about how much her life had changed since Jena had found her in that Dallas diner. The last report she'd heard from Shannon's Elite was nearly half the money had already been returned to its rightful owners. Easton Black believed it wouldn't be more than a couple of weeks for the rest.

She was surrounded by a family who loved her, friends who made her laugh, and two wonderful men who she wanted to spend the rest of her life with. After all the years of being on the run, she'd finally found home.

The buzzer sounded, letting all the players know the round had ended.

She stood and dusted herself off, adjusting her helmet.

Over the loud speaker, a voice announced, "The last person standing is Ethel O'Leary. She's awarded five points for winning this round. In second place, Emmett Stone. He's awarded four points. In third, Erica Strange. Three points. In fourth, Carrie Dixon. Two points. In fifth—"

Matt and Sean ran up to here and gave her a hug.

"Did I hear right? Was I in fourth place?"

"You heard right," Matt said, smiling. He and Sean both wore bright yellow vests, indicating they were security and officials of the game. "We saw what you did."

"Or better said, what you didn't do," Sean said. "You had her, Carrie. Why didn't you take the shot?"

"Believe me, I will next time," she said with a grin. "Call it my newbie mistake."

"I wish I could work the park this next round to see you in action," Matt said. "But Sean and I have to go help run the children's games at Lover's Beach."

"How long before the next round?" she asked.

"Ten minutes," Sean said. "After that one, we'll break for lunch. This afternoon the team challenges begin."

"Do either of you know where Josh or Jacob are?" She wanted to tell them how well she'd done in the last round, although they likely already knew since it had gone out over the loud speaker. But a good-luck kiss from each of them might help in the next round. She might even end up winning. Kisses from them definitely couldn't hurt.

"They worked the overnight shift, filling in for Jaris and Chance. Jaris's dog Sugar delivered eight beautiful puppies, I'm told," Matt said. "I bet Josh and Jacob are asleep."

Sean shook his head. "I just talked to the sheriff. He said they are pulling a double. They're over at Lover's Beach supervising the kid's games right now. Since no cars are allowed on the streets in town, most are parked there and by Silver Spoon Bridge. The ones by the bridge are fine, but a few by the beach have been splattered in paint by some of the kids. Happens every year because some people park too close to the playing field for the kids."

"I'm not surprised Josh and Jacob are still up even though they worked all night. No one gets much sleep during paintball." Matt turned to her. "Carrie, you won't have time to get to Lover's Beach and back before the next round, but I'll let your guys know you want to see them."

"Ask them if they would meet me for lunch." The local restaurants, including Phong's Wok, were catering all the meals, which were served under the big tent behind the Dream Hotel.

"We'll do."

"Jena was asking about you," Sean said. "You've got time to get to the information desk before the next round."

"Good idea," she said. "I can't wait to tell her about having Ethel in my crosshairs. Next time, I won't hesitate to pull the trigger."

"That's a Dixon for you," Sean said.

"She's my sister." Matt smiled. "What else would you expect?"

* * * *

Carrie walked into the lobby of the Dream Hotel. It was filled with players and volunteers. The information desk was to the left of the front door. Jena and two other women were fielding questions by the participants. One of the women held a baby and the other looked like she was going to deliver one very soon.

Jena waved her over when she finished with the two young women gamers. She got up and came around the desk. "I'd hug you, but I don't want to get paint on my clothes."

"I don't blame you."

"I heard your name on the loudspeaker. You're doing great, Carrie."

"I'm having so much fun. I just wish I'd taken Ethel out when I had the chance."

"You had a chance?" an attractive woman behind her asked. Wearing paintball gear, her long dark hair was pulled back in a ponytail.

"Carrie, this is Phoebe Wolfe," Jena said. "She's quite the player herself."

"But I've never had Ethel in my sights." Phoebe shook her hand. "Are you sure you've never played paintball before, Carrie?"

The two women who had been helping Jena at the information desk came up and joined them.

"Yes. I'm sure this is my first time," she said. "I'm a total newbie."

"And you took fourth place in that last round," the woman with the baby said. "I'm Amber Stone."

"I'm Carrie. Pleased to meet you." She gazed at the little boy in Amber's arms. "What's his name?"

"Richard Trevor, but his dads and I call him Ricky."

"He's beautiful."

Amber smiled. "Carrie, this is my sister, Belle. She's going to have her own bundle of joy any day now."

"This excitement may bring it on," Belle said, smiling. "I'm ready to meet my little girl."

"So are her brothers, I bet," Phoebe said. "Where are Juan and Jake?"

"With all the other boys and girls over at Lover's Beach. Juan can't wait for the big free-for-all where all players ten and older finally get to play the real thing."

"They have to be ten to play?" she asked.

Jena nodded. "Children under ten are only allowed to play with water pistols in their own area."

"Amber, where do you want all the ribbons?" Another woman walked up to them, carrying a box.

"On the table," Amber said. "Everyone, this is Grace Summers. She's our new psychologist at the Boys Ranch."

Grace had long, auburn hair and a warm smile. "Nice to meet you."

The five-minute warning sounded, alerting everyone that the next round was about to start.

"It was nice meeting everyone," she said. "Time to go find Ethel O'Leary."

They all laughed.

She and Phoebe left the hotel together.

"Carrie, have you chosen a team to be on for the team event?" Phoebe asked.

"No. I was actually thinking about sitting out that round."

"A player with your skills? Not on your life. Be on my team. There are five of us—me, Gretchen, Erica, Kaylyn, and your archenemy, Ethel. I know for sure they would love to have you on our team. We call ourselves 'The Pistol Packing Mamas.'"

"I'd love to be on your team, but I don't have any kids." She'd never allowed herself to even think about starting a family in the past. But now, after Josh and Jacob had told her how much they loved her, she was imagining what it would like to have a child with them, a child she could be a mother to. In the back of her mind she saw her mother's dark locks. *I wish I had more memories of her.*

"Being a mother is not a requirement. In fact none of us have children, though my guys and I are trying and I believe so are Erica and Kaylyn."

"Not Gretchen?" she asked.

Phoebe laughed. "You'll meet her soon. She's Ethel's age. Besides, she's like a mother to Scott and Eric Knight, and is acting grandmother to their new baby girl. I better say good-bye for now, Carrie, because I may have to shoot you."

"If I don't shoot you first."

Phoebe grinned. "This round is one on one. We're foes until the buzzer sounds. See you on the battlefield."

She watched Phoebe run past one of the dragon statues, and then she rushed to the same park bench where she'd seen Ethel earlier.

Smiling, she stretched out on the ground and waited.

* * * *

Willie looked down at his cell's screen. *Trollinger.*

He let the call go to voicemail. *Again.*

Trollinger had called eleven times in the last few hours. He had more important things to do than to explain to her why he hadn't killed Simmons yet. The fact was, the two men he'd seen with Carrie the day before had been on night watch for the paintball event, not Simmons and his blind sidekick. His information had been wrong about who would be working the shift. No worries. One thing he'd learned a very long time ago, flexibility was crucial to his survival.

He got out of his car and walked to the door of his target's house. The Simmons business would have to come later.

The old lady and little girl were alone inside. *Perfect.*

Chapter Nineteen

Standing by the shoreline with all the supplies, Josh helped five-year-old Jake reload his water pistol. "Which color do you want now?" The kids were allowed to use water that was tinted with food coloring, with a warning to their parents that it might stain their clothes.

"Red, please," the little cowboy said politely. Belle, Sean, and Corey Blue had adopted Jake, as well as Juan. The three of them were doing a wonderful job bringing up the two boys. He was sure they would do the same with their little girl that was on the way.

Jake ran off into the crowd looking like a clown from all the bright spots of food coloring on his white T-shirt, laughing the whole way.

A few feet to his left, Jacob was bent down talking to Daniel, one of the orphan kids from the Boys Ranch.

"You're leading the games, Daniel. Hurry up and get your gun refilled."

"I want blue this time, Mr. Jacob. It shows up better."

Jacob handed the plastic pistol back to the boy. "Here you go. Go get 'em."

Daniel joined the other drenched children on the beach.

"You tired?" he asked Jacob.

"Some, but I wouldn't miss this for the world."

"Me either. Reminds me of you and I when we were boys having our water fights at Mom and Dad's house."

Jacob laughed. "Guns. Balloons. Buckets. But the best was the time we used the hose, remember?"

"How could I forget? I meant to drown you but ended up soaking Mom."

Jacob smiled. "I was sure you and I were in big trouble. But when she grabbed the hose and turned it on us laughing, the game was on. And when Uncle Hiro drove up, she shot him full on. What a day that was. One of the best."

"Yes, it was." Josh scanned the group of kids and saw Jaris and Chance headed his way from the parking lot. Chance had his service dog Annie on a lead.

"Thanks, fellas, for filling in for us last night," Jaris said. "We really appreciate it."

"Of course," Jacob said. "You needed to be with Sugar. How many puppies did she have?"

"Eight," Chance said. "Four males and four females. Kaylyn says if you guys want a German shepherd of your own to come out when the puppies are ready to leave their mother and pick one. About two months from now."

"Aren't they all supposed to become service dogs, like Sugar and Annie?" Josh reached down and petted Chance's dog.

"We have other dogs that will be delivering soon," Jaris said. "We can spare one dog. Besides, if it hadn't been for you two, Chance and I wouldn't have even been there. What do you say? Are you ready to become dog owners?"

He looked over at Jacob. "Our house does have a backyard."

"And we know Carrie loves animals."

"Carrie?" Chance grinned. "The three of you are the talk of the town."

"Are we hearing wedding bells?" Jaris teased.

"Let's do it, Josh."

"Damn, you're getting married? Really?" Jaris smiled.

"Maybe, but we haven't asked her yet," Jacob said. "But what I meant by 'let's do it' was let's get the puppy."

"Agreed." Josh shook Jaris's hand. "Thanks, buddy."

"No. Thank you," Jaris said.

"I'm sure you're exhausted." Chance smiled. "Jaris and I will take over here."

"We really want to finish watching this meet, then we'll head home," Jacob said. "Plus we need to reorganize all the supplies before we go."

Jaris shook his head. "Watch the meet. We'll take care of the supplies."

Jaris and Chance walked to the tent where all the buckets of colored water and shelves of extra pistols were.

He and Jacob continued watching the children, running around, squirting each other, and laughing.

"They are playing so well with each other, Jacob. So far today only one scraped knee."

"I wonder if Carrie has any bruises," Jacob said.

"Probably. You don't come in fourth place in a round without getting a few bumps along the way." He hadn't been able to stop thinking about Carrie since their date last night. He and Jacob had told her they loved her. Luckily, she'd told them she loved them, too. "Jacob, I really want to marry her. In fact, I want to marry her and have a bunch of kids of our own. Do you feel the same way?"

Jacob placed his hand on Josh's shoulder. "You know I do. I'm ready to start a family with Carrie. She's the only one for me."

"For us, you mean."

"Yes," Jacob said. "For us. We need to figure out when and where we want to propose to her."

"Yes we do." He saw Matt and Sean walk onto the beach. "Look who just showed up. The two guys we need to ask permission for Carrie's hand. You want to ask them now?"

"No time like the present," Jacob said. "Hey, guys. Over here."

"Did you hear about Carrie placing in the last round?" Sean asked.

He smiled. "Fourth place. The girl is a natural."

"We're here to take over," Matt said. "You two deserve some sleep."

"Thanks," he said. "But before we go we'd like to talk to you and Sean about something."

"Sure. What is it?"

Carrie has only been in town a few days. "How are Matt and Sean going to react?"

"React to what?" Sean and Matt asked in unison.

"Did I say that out loud? I didn't mean to. How do I begin? Jacob and I want to ask for your permission for your daughter's...I mean your sister's...Damn it, Jacob, help me."

"You guys know Carrie," Jacob blurted out.

Matt and Sean laughed.

"Yes, we know her," Matt said.

Sean grinned. "What about her?"

"You're not going to make this easy on us, are you?" he asked.

"Not a chance," Matt stated with a smile.

"Okay. Here it is. I love Carrie and so does Jacob."

"I do love her," Jacob confessed. "I've never loved anyone as much as Carrie. She's the woman of mine and Josh's dreams."

"So you love her. Anyone can see that," Sean said, not giving them an inch.

Matt teased, "You don't need mine or Sean's permission for that. You can love her all you want. All we ask is that you are good to her. Anything else you wanted to ask us, guys?"

He turned to Jacob. "On three? Together?"

Jacob nodded.

In unison they said, "One. Two. Three. We want to marry Carrie."

In a serious tone Matt said, "Sean and I need to talk about this."

The two men stepped away, speaking in tones too low for him to make out their words.

"They're killing me," Jacob said.

"Me, too."

Matt and Sean came back.

"On three, like we agreed," Matt said to Sean.

"One. Two. Three. Our answer is 'yes.' Welcome to the family, guys." Matt and Sean slapped them on the back.

Josh couldn't stop smiling. "Now all we have to do is ask Carrie."

"Any ideas when you'll do that?" Sean asked.

"Soon," Jacob said. "But we want to make sure we do it right."

"Yes, we do," Josh said, thinking about all the possibilities of time and place that might work. "We want to make it special for Carrie, something to remember forever."

"I thought Matt and I were hopeless romantics," Sean said. "But you two take the top prize."

* * * *

On the ground next to the Mother Dragon statue, Carrie felt her heart thudding in her chest. According to the last announcement, only three players remained in this round—her and two others. She had no doubt that one of the other two was Ethel O'Leary. *I'm coming after you, Ethel.* She wanted to bring back the trophy to her family.

She heard a twig snap. Looking north, she saw a player crawling west across the ground. Was it Ethel? Too far to be sure. She squinted, looking through her scope. She had a clear shot. But the distance was farther than any shot she'd tried. Would she hit her opponent? Once she fired her location would be revealed. She only had one chance.

And then her newbie luck kicked in again. The player stood and fired at someone nearby, giving her a chance to move closer.

She scurried along the ground several feet.

"We are down to two players in this round. Ethel O'Leary and Carrie Dixon. Good luck, ladies. May the best player win."

Carrie took aim at the dear woman she had so much respect for. She fired and saw the yellow paint hit the back of Ethel's shirt. A perfect hit.

Ethel turned around and smiled before falling to the ground.

Carrie felt her cell vibrate in her pocket. *Who could that be?*

* * * *

Jacob's mind was swirling with possibilities to pop the question to Carrie.

"Go get some sleep, guys. You deserve it," Matt said.

"Hold on," Sean interrupted. "Matt, take a look at what just came over the ROC from Grayson and Ross."

Matt brought out the tablet that all members of Shannon's Elite carried with them at all times. "Fuck, the bastard was in Money yesterday."

"What bastard?" Josh asked.

"Willie Mayfield, the crooked minister who killed my parents and kidnapped Carrie."

* * * *

Carrie brought her cell up to her ear. "Hello?"

"You didn't think you could escape me forever, did you?" A voice like a sledgehammer slammed into her eardrum. *His voice.*

"What do you want, Willie?" She closed her eyes and saw the black smoke of her past swirling in her mind.

"What I've always wanted. I want my money and I want you."

"Go to hell."

"Someday, maybe. But right now I'm visiting with the sweetest woman and her little grandchild, Kimmie."

The earth seemed to quake underneath her. "Don't you dare hurt them, you son of a bitch, or I'll kill you."

"That's the fire I remember. Come now. Alone. I know you're at the southwest corner of the park, correct?"

"How can you know that?"

"I have my resources. You have exactly two minutes to get here. You better start running now before someone gets hurt."

The line went dead.

She jumped up and bolted off the playing field.

"What are you doing, Carrie?" Ethel shouted after her. "You'll be disqualified."

"Ethel, call 9-1-1," she yelled back. "Jena's house. Now."

* * * *

Josh read the message on Matt's device.

"Brock and Cooper connected the dots on Carrie's list of churches," Sean said. "They have the current alias he's using. He met with Trollinger in Denver last week and has been in a hotel over in Money for the last few days."

Money, Colorado, was less than a twenty-minute drive away. A primal desire to protect Carrie exploded inside Josh. "We've got to find her. Now."

"Since we can't drive because the streets are blocked off, let's split up," Matt said. "We'll make more ground. Sean and I will take West Street. You two go down East."

Sean was typing away on his device. "I've notified the rest of Shannon's Elite to be on the lookout for Willie and Carrie. Hopefully he's still in Money and not Destiny."

"Let's go." Without another word, Jacob began running to town.

With adrenaline coursing through his veins, Josh ran beside him, praying they would find Carrie still playing paintball—safe.

* * * *

Carrie ran through the front door.

"We're all in here, my darlin'." Willie's pleasant tone sickened her. He was a monster. "In the kitchen."

She raced to the room where Janet had just cooked her breakfast this morning. It seemed like a lifetime ago. The first thing she saw was the dear woman lying on the floor, her body sprawled out on the tile, unmoving.

Willie stood by the sink with a horrific smile plastered across his face. He had a gun holstered to his side.

Running, then kneeling down beside Janet, she screamed, "What have you done to her, you bastard?" Her head was reeling and the smoke in her mind thickened, choking the very life out of her.

"I didn't shoot her, Carrie. Just punched her in the face."

She checked for Janet's pulse and found it.

In a rage, she jumped up and bolted to him, pounding on his chest. "Where's Kimmie?"

Willie slapped her across the face so hard she fell backward to the floor.

"You son of a bitch, where is she?"

Willie stood over her, smiling. "Kimmie is upstairs playing. You shouldn't be so upset, Carrie. Everything will be just fine. I'll get my money and you and I can leave this hellhole town."

"I would never go anywhere with you."

"Oh yes you will go, if you love that little girl."

* * * *

Jacob looked in every direction for Carrie but still couldn't find her. His gut tightened. *She is supposed to be here playing the game.*

"There's Ethel," Josh said, running beside him. "Maybe she's seen Carrie."

"This is an emergency." Ethel looked up from her cell as they stepped next to her. "Boys, Carrie is in trouble. She told me to call 9-1-1 and ran to Jena's house. I have the sheriff on the phone. Go. Run."

* * * *

Still on the floor with Willie bent over her, Carrie heard Kimmie upstairs singing to her music playing loudly on her stereo. *Thank God, she can't hear what is going on.*

I brought my monster to the steps of this house, the home of the only family I've ever known.

She would make sure Willie left Destiny, the place where she'd found true love with Josh and Jacob. It broke her heart to think she would never see them again, but she had no other choice. Leaving with Willie now was the only way to make sure Kimmie was safe.

"I'll go with you," she said, staring into his evil eyes and praying he would leave without harming Kimmie. "Let's go now. You and me."

"That's my girl." Willie pressed his knee into her chest, making it difficult to breathe. "First things first. Where's my money?"

"It's not here." *The truth.* "I put it in a safe place back in Texas." *A lie.*

He slapped her across the face again, and the smoke thickened in her mind. "Lies, you little slut. Tell me where my money is now if you value your life." The instant he reached for his gun, she kicked him with all her might in the groin.

He groaned and doubled over on top of her, pinning her to the floor with his weight.

I need to get to Kimmie. I need to get her away to safety.

With every ounce of strength left inside her, she tried to wiggle out from under him, clawing at his face with her fingernails. The smoke was so thick it choked every thought that came across in her mind.

"Fucking bitch!" He wrapped his fingers around her neck and began squeezing until she could no longer breathe. "I want my money, whore. I want it now. Give it to me. It's mine."

Trying to fight him off, she remembered telling Ethel to call 9-1-1. *Someone must be coming. Kimmie must be safe.*

She realized her life was slipping away. Willie continued choking her, but his screams seemed distant, fading with each second that passed.

She closed her eyes, and all she could see was the smoke. *The damn smoke.* It had haunted her year after year, crushing all her hopes and dreams. Through the smoke, she heard Josh and Jacob's voices. They loved her, and she loved them.

The smoke vanished and images of Josh and Jacob floated in front of her.

* * * *

Hearing Willie ranting, Josh bolted into the kitchen with Jacob. When he saw the fucker on top of Carrie choking her, an all-consuming fury blasted out of him. No thinking. Just raw, primal action. He and Jacob charged, knocking Willie off of Carrie and flattening the bastard to the ground.

Willie pulled out a gun, but Jacob was able to wrestle it away from the motherfucker.

Josh pounded his fists into the bastard's face, again and again, until Willie's head fell back against the tiles with a loud thud, the asshole's eyes swollen shut and his breathing shallow.

Vibrating with pure rage, it took all Josh's willpower to stop from killing the man.

"You got him?" Jacob asked, his face tight and his eyes dark.

"Yes. Check on Carrie." He kept hold of Willie just in case the bastard regained consciousness and glanced back at Carrie. He spotted Jena's mother lying on the floor across the room. The only thing his eyes had focused on was Carrie when he'd run into the kitchen. Clearly, Carrie wasn't the only one Willie had harmed.

"Carrie's breathing, Josh. The color in her face is returning. She's opening her eyes."

Thank God. "Check on Jena's mom."

Jacob moved quickly to the fallen woman. "Janet is breathing but has a big gash on her forehead. She and Carrie both need medical attention now." Jacob brought out his cell, but before he could make a call, Sheriff Wolfe and Doc Ryder came in with their guns drawn. Doc also carried his medical bag. Josh recalled Ethel had called 9-1-1. That was the reason the sheriff and Doc had come so quickly. More would be arriving soon.

"Any other intruders?" the sheriff asked, tossing over a pair of handcuffs.

"Don't know, but I don't think so." Josh rolled the unconscious bastard over on his stomach and clamped the sheriff's bracelets around his wrists.

Matt, Sean, and Jena rushed in with their guns out also.

"Where's my daughter?" Jena asked frantically. "Where's Kimmie?"

"Upstairs," Jacob answered. "I can hear her singing, can you?"

Jena didn't respond, but she, Matt, and Sean shot up the stairs.

Easton Black and Jaris Simmons came in with their guns out also, followed by Paris, Doc's wife and a physician herself. Paris wore paintball gear but held a Glock instead of a play weapon. Everyone in Destiny carried guns. It was the norm here, especially since the war with Trollinger's brother had begun.

Black and Sheriff Wolfe left to check out the rest of the house for any other intruders. Doc took Carrie's blood pressure and listened to her heartbeat through his stethoscope while Paris did the same with Janet.

"Carrie is okay," Doc said. "Pressure is fine and so is her pulse."

"Janet's pressure and pulse are normal, too," Paris said. "But she needs stitches and she also has a concussion."

"We need to get both of these women back to the hospital for further care," Doc said.

Willie stirred and began cursing. "Fuck you, assholes. This isn't the end. Cindy Trollinger will see to it."

Jaris bent down next to Josh.

"Simmons?" Willie spat. "You're a dead man. Enjoy today because it won't be long before you have a bullet planted between your eyes."

"Shut the fuck up." Josh punched Willie in the face again. It wasn't what a good guy did, but he didn't feel like being good right now. "You're lucky I don't slit your throat for hurting Carrie, motherfucker. Be smart and keep quiet."

The asshole nodded and shut up.

"Go to Carrie, Josh," Jaris said. "I got this bastard. He's not going anywhere."

Josh knelt down beside Carrie. She was coming to.

Jacob was on the other side of her, holding her hand. "We nearly lost her, Josh."

"But we didn't," he said as relief replaced the intense rage inside him. "Carrie's okay. Doc said so."

"What's going on, Josh?" Carrie's voice was raspy and her throat was red where Willie's hands had been. Her eyes were completely open now. "Why are all these people here?"

"Just relax." He could tell she was a little confused. "What's the last thing you remember, sweetheart?"

"Paintball, I think. Didn't I shoot Ethel?"

Chapter Twenty

Jacob held the door for Katy, Carrie's nurse, who was bringing her back from the X-ray room. Josh adjusted Carrie's pillow as Katy helped her into the hospital bed.

"Doc will be here shortly," Katy said. "If you need anything, Carrie, just use the buzzer."

"I will. Thanks."

Katy left.

He and Josh stood on opposite sides of the bed, taking Carrie's hands.

"Tell me again, what happened after I shot Ethel?" The panic in her tone hadn't gone away.

He and Josh recounted all the events to her one more time. He believed she kept asking to hear it again in the hopes it would jog her memory. But so far, it hadn't.

"You're completely safe, angel," he said, touching her on the cheek. "Willie is in jail."

"Are you sure Kimmie is okay?"

"She's fine. She has no idea about what happened."

"Good," Carrie said. "And what about Janet?"

He squeezed her hand. "Janet is fine. She got stitched up and Doc and Paris are going to keep her overnight for observation since she did suffer a concussion."

"What a relief." She sighed. "Why can't I remember any of it?"

He saw her eyes well up.

"I'm just no good for you," she blurted out, and the tears streamed down her face. "I'm a broken mess. What if I keep losing memories?

What happens when I can't remember how much you mean to me? What then? You deserve someone better, someone who is whole. Not me. My heart is ripping apart. I want you both so very much. I love you, but I know that I'm wrong for you. I have to let you go. I need to leave Destiny before I cause more pain."

She covered her face with her hands and sobbed.

Jacob pulled her into his chest, holding her tight. "It's going to be okay, Carrie."

"No," she said. "It can't be."

Josh put his arms around both of them. "Sweetheart, it's the three of us now. You're not alone anymore. You'll never be alone again."

"No more talk about you leaving," he said, remembering how Josh had helped him through his darkest hours. Together, he and Josh would do the same for her. "We will fight this together."

"But what if—"

"Shh." He placed his finger to her lips. "Do you trust me and Josh?"

"With all my heart."

"Then believe us when we say everything is going to be okay."

"I want to believe you, but I still feel so confused. I'm the reason Willie came to Destiny. What if he'd hurt Kimmie?"

"He didn't, angel. She's safe. Jena's mom is safe. And you're safe. Willie will pay for all his crimes. He's going to prison for the rest of his life."

"Even so, Jacob, I still don't understand why I can't remember something so horrible."

"That's why we're here, to figure out why. And I'm sure we will."

As if on cue, Doc entered the room with Sam O'Leary. "How's my patient doing?"

Carrie sat up in the bed. "Better. I think my voice is almost back to normal."

"By tomorrow your vocal cords should be completely healed," Doc said. "I asked Sam to join me to discuss your memory loss, Carrie."

"That's what I was just discussing with Josh and Jacob," she said. "There's something terribly wrong with me."

Sam moved to the side of the bed and leaned forward, smiling, reminding Jacob of the first time he'd met the man. Sam had the kindest face he'd ever seen.

"Carrie," Sam said. "Doc Ryder's tests have shown there is nothing medically wrong with you."

She sighed. "Then it's official. I'm must be crazy."

"Absolutely not, young lady. And you and I can get to the bottom of this if you will let me help you."

She turned to him and Josh. "Do you really believe he can help me?"

Josh kissed her on the cheek. "Yes, sweetheart. I know he can."

"Sam helped me out of my darkness, Carrie," he said, taking her hand. She'd survived so much. She would survive this, too. "He will help you."

Carrie took a deep breath and looked right into Sam's eyes. "Okay. When?"

"Doc, when are you releasing her?" Sam asked.

"Right now. She's free to go home, but I do want her taking it easy for a few days."

"Good," Sam said. "Carrie, I will see you in my office first thing tomorrow morning at nine."

"I'll be there."

Doc and Sam left.

"I'm proud of you, angel," Jacob said. She was strong, much stronger than she realized.

"I'm proud of you, too," Josh added. "Very proud. I can't even imagine how difficult this is for you."

"I'm a little scared to go see Sam," she admitted. "I'm not sure what he might uncover, but I want to stop running away from my demons. I want the three of us to have a chance for a future."

"It's more than a chance, sweetheart," Josh said. "It's a fact."

Jacob nodded, completely of the same mind. "No more talk about you leaving, understand?"

"Yes, Masters. I love you and I do understand."

* * * *

Carrie leaned back on Sam's sofa. "What am I supposed to do exactly? How does therapy work?"

Sam sat in the chair next to the sofa. "Carrie, you don't have to be nervous. Just consider me an old grandpa listening to his granddaughter."

She grinned. "Is that ethical in your profession?"

He laughed. "I'm semi-retired. I do things my own way. Or should I say, 'the Destiny way.' One thing I can tell you for certain is if you trust me and are honest with me, together we will find your path. Tell me about your past."

She took a deep breath and began recounting every detail she could recall to Sam. It didn't take long, since she had so many gaps. She told him about Willie beating her, about the nightmares of smoke. She confessed being unable to recall what her parents looked like, and so many other things she'd lost. Mrs. Kearns was the only person from all the churches Willie had conned that she could remember.

"So you had no memory loss from the time you escaped Willie until yesterday?"

"That's true."

"Carrie, I believe that your predator is the one who triggered all your memory loss," Sam said. "That night he beat you after you told him about your nightmare was the first incident of memory loss. It was nearly a week later before your memory returned. The next time he whipped your back with his belt because you cried in front of him. That's the thread in your past that sticks out to me. But I believe your mind began blocking out the worst of his cruelty toward you. I'm sure he beat you many more times than you can remember. Have you ever heard of post-traumatic stress disorder?"

"PTSD? Yes. I thought that had to do with how some soldiers dealt with the horrors of the battlefield."

"That's true, but you faced your own horrors, your own battlefield. And you were just a child when your war began." Sam brought out a pocket watch, which hung from a chain.

"Don't tell me you plan on hypnotizing me?"

"I'd like to try if you are willing, but I'm not going to use my watch, Carrie." Sam smiled. "That's mainly done in the movies. I just wanted to check the time."

She laughed, feeling a little nervous. "I've never been hypnotized before."

"And you might not be today either. We'll just give it a try and see how it goes. If we succeed, you will remember everything about this session. There's nothing to worry about, Carrie. Even hypnotized, you cannot be made to do anything that you don't want to do."

Sam dimmed the lights.

She shifted on the sofa, getting into a more comfortable position.

"Just relax. Close your eyes and concentrate on your breathing. In and out. Nice and slow. Imagine the waves of the ocean coming in and going out. Nice and slow. The color of the sand darkening as the water covers the tiny particles and then lightening as the sun warms the beach. Breathe in as the waves come in. And breathe out as the waves go out. Feel the sun on your face and the warm water around your body. You are very relaxed."

She continued listening to Sam's soothing voice. She felt like she was floating.

"Just let your feet relax, and your legs relax. Feel your hips and waist softening. Every bit of tension melting away. No fears. No worries. Feel your chest relaxing, and your arms relaxing. Breathing in and out. Your shoulders relaxing, and your neck and head relaxing. Feel your entire body relaxing, all over as the waves move in and out."

Sam continued talking, guiding her into the air, flying up to a cloud, laughing and full of joy. She was at peace. No stress. No worries. No cares. Totally relaxed.

"Carrie, you are resting comfortably in a deep, peaceful state of sleep, going deeper and faster and deeper and faster all of the time, until I bring you back. You will only accept those suggestions which are for your benefit, and that you are willing to accept. Know you are safe."

She did feel safe. Completely safe.

"Now, visualize a curtain in front of you. Feel the fabric."

In her mind, she saw a red velvet curtain that hung from a large rod.

"Behind this curtain is one of your memories, Carrie. It's a pleasant memory. You haven't seen it in a very long time, but you know it's there, waiting for you to rediscover it. When you part the curtain, you will see the past but you won't be in the past. You will enjoy the happy memory and when you return from this place you will remember every detail. Open the curtain, Carrie."

Completely at peace, she opened the curtain and saw Matt and Sean when they were boys. They were playing hide-and-seek with her and some other children.

"What do you see, Carrie?"

As the memory grew brighter, she told him every detail. "I'm behind a tree, but Sean found me. I give him a hug. I hear my mom call my name. I run to her. I see her face. I remember what she looks like. She looks like me. We have the same color eyes. My dad is standing beside her with his arms around her shoulder." Her gut tightened when she saw a younger version of Willie walk up beside them. "Go away."

"Breathe, Carrie. Feel the water. In and out. The sun on your face. Nothing can hurt you. You can remember everything, but know you are safe."

She saw the black smoke swirling around Willie, but she wasn't afraid. "I'm safe."

"Yes, you are. What do you see now?"

"A fire. Willie is grabbing me and taking me down into a tunnel. The smoke is all around us. I'm coughing and coughing. My eyes burn."

Sam guided her to more doors and curtains, returning all her lost memories to her.

"One final door, Carrie, before I bring you back. This is the door to yesterday, when you were playing paintball and shot Ethel. Open the door and see what happened."

"I answered my cell and heard Willie's voice." All the time she'd lost came back to her. Yelling for Ethel to call 9-1-1. Running into the kitchen and finding Janet on the floor. Kicking Willie in the groin when he reached for his gun. Trying to break free from the bastard when he was choking her. "I saw Josh and Jacob come to my rescue. They saved me."

"You will remember every memory you saw, Carrie, but always know that you are safe. Now, I'm going to bring you back. I'm going to count from one to five, and at the count of five you will be feeling wide awake, fully alert, and completely refreshed. One. You're feeling more awake. Two. Even more awake. Three."

When Sam said five, she was completely awake. She sat up. "Oh Sam, you did it."

"You did it, Carrie. You did the hard work. I just guided you."

Thrilled beyond belief, she leapt from the sofa and hugged him. "You gave me back my memories. I remember everything. The faces of my mother and father. I even remember Sean now. Such a sweet boy. He always treated me like a sister. Still does. Oh my God. They're all back. Even the bad ones, but they can't hurt me anymore.

I'm free. Josh and Jacob are in the other room waiting for me. Do you mind if they come in so we can tell them everything?"

Sam gave her a kiss on the cheek. "I'll get them for you."

He opened the door. "Guys, Carrie wants to see you."

They rushed in with questioning looks on their faces.

She felt happy tears streaming down her face, telling her why they seemed concerned. "I remember. I remember."

Josh put his arm around her shoulders.

"You okay, angel?" Jacob asked, taking her hands.

"Better than okay," she said, smiling. "I remember. I have my memories back. All of them."

"That's wonderful." Josh kissed her. "I love you so much."

"And I love you," she said, bubbling over with joy.

Jacob pulled her in close. "I knew Sam would help you."

"She's the one who helped herself," Sam said. "Just like you did, Jacob."

"Thanks, Sam." Jacob pressed his mouth to her lips. "I love you, angel."

"And I love you. I can't wait to tell Sean I remember him."

"Then we better get going," Josh said, leading her to the door.

"Thank you, Sam." She looked at the dear man. "Same time tomorrow?"

"You got it, Carrie."

Chapter Twenty-One

Carrie ran into her family's home, anxious to tell them about how Sam had helped her. Josh and Jacob were by her side when she walked into the living room and saw everyone.

Janet sat on the sofa next to Gary, who was holding her hands.

"They released you, Mom." Carrie rushed to Janet and gave her a hug. "I'm so sorry that this happened to you because of me."

"Because of you? Hush, Carrie. You had nothing to do with that madman's action. I'm just thankful he was caught and put where he belongs."

"Carrie," Jena said, standing between Matt and Sean. "We're not telling Kimmie the real reason mom was in the hospital. We told her she fell. I don't want her to be scared, and we'll tell her when she's old enough to understand."

"I totally agree with you. I certainly know what it's like to be scared when you're little. No child should have to be scared. Where is my precious niece?"

"Where else?" Sean grinned. "She's outside playing with Happiness. Not a care in the world."

"Sean, I need to tell you something," she said, grabbing Josh and Jacob's hands for support. "I didn't tell you the truth when I said I remembered you."

"I know, sweetheart. I suspected you didn't want to hurt my feelings."

"You're right, but I remember you now. I remember everything. How you treated me like a sister, just like now."

"I'm thrilled to hear that, Carrie. It means so much to me."

"And Matt, Sam helped me get all my memories back. I remember what mom and dad looked like. They weren't all bad."

"They weren't. They were just under Willie's evil spell."

"You remember everything about your past?" Jena asked.

"Yes. The good and the bad. Sam helped me rediscover all of my memories. I'm going to continue seeing him for a while, but I feel whole for the first time in my life. And that's thanks to all of you. Jena, you found me and brought me back to Destiny. You gave me Matt and Sean back. And a beautiful niece." She turned to Janet and Gary. "And a new mother and father." She squeezed Josh and Jacob's hands. "And because of all of you, I now know what it is to be truly loved. And I love you all so very much."

* * * *

After eating the delicious meal that his mom and dad had dropped off earlier, Josh washed the dishes. Matt was drying them and Sean was putting them away. Gary wiped the table and Jacob swept the floor.

Carrie was with Jena and Janet in the living room, enjoying their dessert and coffee. Kimmie had gotten her bath and had been tucked into bed.

"I had no idea that your dad made anything but Asian food," Matt said, taking the last dish from him and rinsing it off.

Sean nodded. "Those burgers were delicious. I've never tasted anything quite like them before."

"Don't you dare say that outside these walls," he warned them, knowing how secretive his dad was about his burgers. "He must consider you family now because that's a first."

After the kitchen was completely clean, Josh and the other men joined the women in the living room.

"Was Ethel happy that she won that last round of paintball I was in because I had to leave?" Carrie asked, sipping on her coffee.

"Actually no," Jena said. "She wanted you to be declared the winner, but the judges decided to uphold the rules. When you left the gaming area you forfeited, I'm sorry to say."

"I'm not. The first time I didn't shoot her, and the second time I felt so guilty. I just love Ethel's spunk. I want to be just like her."

"Sis, you're well on your way," Matt said.

"Thanks, brother." Carrie shook her head. "What I forgot to ask was if any of you figured out how Willie found me."

"With the help of Cindy Trollinger," Sean said. He told them about the connection between Trollinger and Willie, how they'd met in Denver. "Thank God, that bastard is behind bars. Black's been able to get some good information out of him that may help us locate Trollinger. He's trying to plea bargain but it won't work."

"You think Trollinger will try to spring Willie?" Gary asked.

"No," Matt said. "It's our understanding that she's even put out a contract on him."

"We had her pinpointed in Berlin two days ago when somehow she was able to vanish off our radar," Jena said. "We still believe she is out of the country, likely using a new alias."

"That's good to hear." Janet leaned into Gary. "It'll give Destiny a chance to catch its breath."

"And it will also give more time for Shannon's Elite to find Trollinger again." Josh believed in the entire team that Black had put together. They had incredible talents and skills. "You'll find her, I have no doubt."

"How long will Willie be in the county jail?" Carrie asked.

"A couple more days, Sis," Matt said. "The FBI is sending some agents to retrieve him."

"I'll just be glad when the bastard is out of here." Jacob put his arm around Carrie.

"I need to face Willie before they take him," she said.

"I don't think that's a very good idea, Carrie," Janet said.

"Neither do I," Gary agreed. "He's caused you too much grief already."

"That's the reason I need to see him. I need to prove to myself that I'm not afraid of him anymore. I've been running my whole life from him. No more."

"Sweetheart, I think that's actually a good idea," Jacob said. "Face your demon head on."

Josh knew that if anyone understood what Carrie had gone through, it was Jacob. "Just promise me that you will talk to Sam about this first, Carrie."

"I promise. I see him first thing in the morning."

* * * *

After speaking with Sam that morning, Carrie felt extremely confident with what she was about to do. She was closing the chapter of her dark past forever.

She stood between Josh and Jacob in Sheriff Jason Wolfe's office, holding their hands.

"Are you three sure about this?" the sheriff asked. "This is quite an unusual request."

"This is something I must do for myself, Sheriff."

"And you two support this?" he asked Josh and Jacob.

"We do." Josh squeezed her hand.

"Sheriff," Jacob said, "this is Carrie's way of ending the darkness of her childhood and embracing her new life with us in Destiny."

"Okay," the sheriff said. "I will take you to the prisoner, but I will be within earshot in case you need me."

"Thank you, Sheriff, for understanding," she said.

The sheriff led them to Willie's cell.

"You fucking whore!" Willie grabbed the bars. "How much of my money have you spent on your two gigolos already?"

Josh and Jacob started to step forward but she put her hands in front of them. "It's okay. I need to handle this."

Even though she could see the protective rage on their faces, they stopped, clearly respecting her wishes.

She turned her attention back to Willie, whose eyes were filled with hate. She no longer feared him. Her monster no longer had claws. "I knew your only concern would be about the money. This was exactly what I expected from an evil, demented man like you. The fact is, Willie, we are returning your money to the churches you stole from. In fact, some of it has already been returned."

"You bitch. That's not possible. I deserve that money. It's mine."

"Oh it is possible," she said softly. "I kept a secret list from you all those years of every church you conned. They were good people. You manipulated them into trusting you. You even used me, claiming I was your little motherless daughter. The lies have come back to haunt you, asshole. And now that the truth is out you will never be able to con anyone again. No one will ever trust you. Not even in prison, where you'll be spending the rest of your miserable life."

"Trollinger will get me out of here," Willie spat. "And when she does I'm coming after you, Carrie. You and your two perverts."

"The way I understand it, she doesn't want to have anything to do with you. And besides, where they're sending you, Trollinger won't be able to find you."

"You lying bitch."

"Enjoy your cage, William." She turned to Josh and Jacob, feeling completely free. "I'm finished here. Let's go."

Willie continued cursing as they left him behind.

Chapter Twenty-Two

"Are you sure this isn't too skimpy?" Carrie asked Jena, staring at her own reflection in the full-length mirror. Halloween was more than a month away, and yet here she was wearing a costume. She had on a little white half shirt that tied in the front that put on exhibit her cleavage, a plaid pleated mini skirt that was shorter than any she'd ever worn before, thigh-high sheer stockings and a pair of red stilettos. "I've never worn anything this revealing in public before."

"I'm sure you haven't." Jena came up beside her. "Look at what I'm wearing. Talk about your little black dress. If I bend over, there will be nothing left for the imagination."

She smiled. "You look really sexy."

"My guys love parading me around the club like this. I'm their prize to show off as they please, but a prize that no one but them can touch. They really get off on it. Yours will, too. Take these. It will enhance your whole look." Jena handed her a pair of glasses with thick black frames and an oversized multicolored lollipop. "Damn, Carrie. You look good."

Getting into the spirit of the night, she asked. "You think I should put my hair up in pigtails?"

"If you think Josh and Jacob would like it, I say go for it."

"I'm pretty sure they would want my hair down." She spun around, excited about the evening. Tonight would be her first night at Phase Four.

"You make a very sexy naughty school girl, Carrie. Your guys are going to be beaming with pride." Jena looked at the time on her cell. "They should be here any moment.

They heard the doorbell.

Jena smiled. "Told you. They're here. Ready for the night of your life?"

She took a deep breath. "I am."

"Wait a couple of minutes before you come out." Jena walked to the bedroom door. "I want to see the look on Josh and Jacob's faces when you make your entrance."

"Thanks for helping me get ready, Jena."

"What are sisters-in-law for?"

She smiled. "You mean sisters."

"Yes. Sisters." Jena walked into the hallway and shut the door.

Carrie took another look at herself in the mirror. Jena was right, she did look sexy. She smiled, feeling her heart pound a little faster in her chest. Anxious to see how the night went, she glanced over at the clock on her nightstand. 11:10 p.m. Jena had told her that the club's biggest crowd showed after getting their kids to bed, thus the late hour. Phase Four was so much more than a BDSM club. It was a place the community gathered, a place where judgment wasn't tolerated, a place where sexuality was prized in all its many forms. A place of total freedom to be whatever you wanted to be.

She walked out of the bedroom for the adventure she'd been dreaming about. And the two men who would be her guides were waiting by the door to escort her to the club.

A leather harness was wrapped around Josh's muscled chest and six-pack abs. The black jeans and military boots reinforced the image of dominance he presented. Jacob wore a black leather vest and pants that exposed his well-built body perfectly. Like Josh, he wore black military boots. They both carried a leather satchel. She had a pretty good idea what was inside the black bags. There was no doubt in her mind who was in control of tonight. Her two Masters were.

"Here she is," Jena announced, standing between Matt and Sean, who were also wearing Dom gear.

Josh's eyes widened. "Wow."

"You really like it?" she asked.

"I sure do, sweetheart."

Jacob smiled. "You look gorgeous, Carrie."

Thrilled with Josh and Jacob's praise, she said, "So do you and Josh. Handsome, I mean."

"Do we all want to ride together?" Sean asked Josh and Jacob. "We can take the Suburban."

Destiny families were like any other in the country. They drove SUVs, ate dinner together, paid bills, had children. But there were a few differences. The people here didn't put any boundaries on what family meant and they weren't afraid to express their sexuality in a variety of ways.

"No thanks, Sean," Jacob said. "We'll be staying later than you three. It's Carrie's first time, so we have a lot planned for her tonight."

A shiver ran up and down her spine as she wondered what he and Josh had in mind for the evening for her.

"Sure thing," Sean said.

"We'll see you at the club, guys." Matt turned to Jena. "Come with us, sub."

Jena smiled and sent her a knowing wink. "Yes, Master."

Matt and Sean led Jena to the entrance to the garage, which was through the kitchen.

When they were alone, Josh pulled Carrie in close and kissed her, getting the first round of tonight's tingles started. "God, you look hot." He spun her around to face Jacob. "Don't you agree?"

"I do," Jacob said and pressed his mouth to her lips. "Let's go, little sub."

"Yes, Master." She smiled, and he smiled back.

"We have set up some surprises for you tonight, angel. Things we've never done with you before." He kissed her again and then opened the door.

As her excitement enlarged inside her, her legs wanted to run to the truck. She didn't but instead remained between Josh and Jacob, her two big bad Doms. They'd saved her, not just from Willie, but from the self-doubt and fear that had manifested as the smoke in her nightmares. The darkness was gone. Her nightmares, too, replaced by wonderful dreams. And because of her two wonderful men and with the help of Sam, her memories were back in place.

When they got to the end of the sidewalk, she stopped by the passenger door of the truck. She could've opened the door herself, but knew the rules they'd set up between each other. So she waited.

Josh grabbed her hand and brought it up to his chest. Having his hot flesh and leather straps of his harness under her fingers felt good.

"We're not driving, sweetheart." Josh smiled. "It's a beautiful Colorado night. The club is only a few blocks away."

"We're walking?" She was shocked to hear that. The only way to Phase Four from here was down South Street, out in the open, where anyone could see how she was dressed. "B–but—"

"But what?" His voice deepened and his eyes grew dark, making her tremble.

She lowered her gaze. "I'm sorry, Master, but I'm more nervous than I thought."

"And?" Jacob said, stroking her hair.

"And I feel exposed wearing this outfit. What if Hiro or Melissa sees me when we pass by the Wok?"

He and Josh laughed.

"They're at their home, angel. Asleep by now. Besides, you look incredible. We like you exposed."

"We want the whole world to see what a beautiful woman we have," Josh added. "Understand?"

"Yes, Master." She remembered what Jena had said about how Doms liked parading subs around the club, prizes to show off. *I'm Josh and Jacob's prize.*

She walked between them, holding their hands. Each step closer to the club increased the butterflies in her belly. She was excited and nervous. What awaited her at Phase Four? What were the special things Josh and Jacob had planned—for her?

As they turned onto South Street, she noted that the protective plastic was still in place on the statues and all the buildings. Once Willie had been locked away, she'd returned to playing paintball. Her squad, the Pistol Packing Mamas, had come out on top of the team round, taking the blue ribbon. That win moved Ethel to the top of the leader board. Carrie sat in the twentieth position, which was pretty good since she'd forfeited one round and had to miss two others. Tomorrow was the closing ceremony, and even though she wouldn't get a trophy she wanted to be there to see Ethel get hers.

She spotted Belle, the pregnant woman she'd met at the paintball information desk, walking with two handsome men, Belle's husbands, no doubt. Belle wore slacks and a green top. The man on her right wore a cowboy hat, jeans, and boots. The one on her right was in a US Marshal's uniform.

Oh God. What if they see me? She took a deep breath, hoping that they wouldn't. *Why didn't I put on a long jacket over this outfit before we left?*

"Hey, guys," Josh waved at them, ruining her chance of remaining inconspicuous. "Nice night for a walk."

"It sure is," the uniformed one said.

"Where are the boys?" Jacob asked.

"Back home," the other man answered, "with Riley, who came by to take care of them while their parents enjoyed a night out."

"Carrie, you look great," Belle said, smiling. "Is this your first time to the club?"

She nodded, feeling better about being seen on the street in her naughty schoolgirl outfit.

"I remember my first time with these two." Belle looked at her husbands with adoring eyes.

"Should you be walking being so far along?" She didn't know much about pregnancy, having been on the run for so long. But she planned on learning more. *One day I want children of my own. With Josh and Jacob.* "Aren't you due any day?"

"Doc says walking is good for me. And who knows? Maybe tonight will be the night I get to hold my baby girl. Have fun at the club."

They passed a few more people on the way to Phase Four, and each encounter only made her more excited. *I'm Josh and Jacob's prize. They are proud to show me off.*

When they got to the front doors of the club, there were people lined up out the door. All wore a variety of BDSM clothing, and in comparison to many of the female subs' dresses, her outfit was almost modest. Almost.

Her nervousness returned in full force. *Am I really ready for this?* She wondered how big the crowd was inside.

The line moved quickly and they were inside the reception area of the club in no time at all.

Unlike the rest of the people who flashed a membership card at the big Dom standing by the door that opened to an expansive hall, Josh and Jacob led her to the reception desk. She still could hear the music from the room beyond, causing her pulse to increase as she filled out the club's paperwork. According to the form, Josh and Jacob, who were already members of the club, were to be her escorts. She was their responsibility.

"You're all set," the Dom behind the desk said, handing Jacob a key. "Enjoy."

They walked into the club. All she could see in every direction were wall-to-wall Doms and subs.

There were four stages, each with scenes being played out.

One was decked out like a pirate ship, complete with cannons, sails, and masts. The three Doms and sub on the platform were dressed for their roles perfectly. One of the Doms even had an eye patch, making her wonder if it was for the scene or for real. The woman was tied to the center mast and the men were flogging her one at a time. The look of ecstasy on the sub's face couldn't be missed.

On the center stage was a cage. The scenery reminded her of a medieval dungeon in many ways. Inside the cage was a male submissive, completely naked. His two Doms were poking him with what appeared to be electric prods. The male sub had that same faraway look as the woman on the other stage.

The other two stages were dimly lit and vacant of people, though they were decorated with one reminding her of a doctor's office and the other a classroom.

At both of the active stages were large audiences watching intently. Others in the club filled the dance floor.

"Let's watch," Jacob said. He and Josh led her to the pirate ship stage.

She noticed several men in white leathers. She'd learned they were called the angels, club Doms who enforced Phase Four's rules and protocols. Until yesterday, when Josh and Jacob had resigned, they had been club Doms. When they'd told her about their decision to quit, she'd asked Jena why she thought they'd done that. Jena had told her that club Doms not only kept the peace at Phase Four, they were also trainers for the club, teaching both Doms and subs about the lifestyle.

After hearing that, Carrie was glad that Josh and Jacob had resigned. She didn't want to share her Doms with anyone. Ever.

The moans of the woman on the pirate stage demanded her full attention, pushing away Carrie's racing thoughts. That's when she recognized who the submissive was. Amber Stone, Belle's sister who had also worked at the information desk with Jena. Amber's three Doms had to be her husbands. The casual onlooker might have missed the care with which they treated Amber, but Carrie saw it with every caress, pinch, and slap. The result was Amber was in that state of warmth and fuzziness that she herself craved. *A state of utter bliss.*

Josh leaned over and said, "Come with us, sub." His commanding tone made her tingle all over.

She followed him and Jacob to the stage that looked like a classroom. When they led her up the stairs onto the platform, her heart thudded like a hummingbird's.

"Look at our sub's face, Jacob." Josh smiled. "She's wondering if we mean to put her on display for the whole club, and that's making her very nervous."

Jacob came up beside her, putting his arm around her. "Are you nervous?"

"Yes, Master." *The truth.* "Do you really want me to do a scene in front of everyone…on my first night at the club?"

"We do. We want to show you off. You'll do great, angel. We'll make sure of it." Jacob led her to one of the student chairs. "Sit."

She obeyed and watched her two Doms empty out their satchels on the table by the teacher's desk. They were meticulous in spreading out the toys and paraphernalia for tonight's fun. Jacob held up a scary-looking black paddle before placing it on the table's surface.

She found the desk unusual. At each corner was a metal post with an attached ring. Four posts and rings no doubt meant to attach clamps and cuffs to in order to restrain submissives.

She was excited, proud, and so deliciously nervous.

Josh walked over to a panel and switched on the lights of the stage. Keeping her eyes locked on Josh and Jacob was the only thing that held her in place as she could hear people moving to the seats in front of the stage. *Our stage. Oh God. I'm really doing this.*

Josh came over. "Play your part, sub. Put those glasses back on and hold up the lollipop."

"Yes, Master." She didn't dare break focus from him and Jacob. In her mind, she pretended this was a classroom and they were her teachers. Actually, they were. They'd taught her so much and now the nightmare smoke was gone forever. She felt strong and powerful.

Whole. And with them, she could always embrace everything feminine inside her.

Jacob came over, carrying a blindfold and a pair of earphones attached to his cell.

Josh addressed their audience. "Tonight Master Jacob and I will—"

"Focus on me, angel," Jacob said as Josh continued setting up the scene for those watching. "This is your first public scene. Relax. Josh and I know what to do. I'm going to remove two of your senses, sub. That will allow you to let go of your fears much faster in this context."

As he continued telling her about what he was about to do to her, she felt her anxiety fade and her anticipation sharpen.

He removed the black-framed glasses and placed the blindfold on her, taking away her vision as he'd promised.

"I've selected some wonderful songs for you. Focus on them. Listen to their beats. This will drown out all the sounds around us. Understand?"

She nodded.

He placed the earphones in her ears. The song playing from his music list was an instrumental with a heavy bass line. The hypnotic beat lulled her quickly.

She felt four hands on her—Josh and Jacob's. They guided her out of the seat and led her forward. They bent her over the desk until she was on her tiptoes. Then they stretched out her arms. She felt leather around her wrists. Being attached to two of the desk's metal posts kept her from moving her arms.

Oh God. How many people are watching?

She took a deep breath and focused on the beat of Jacob's song. *Boom. Boom. Boom.*

She was on stage, on display, trembling. When they lifted her skirt, she tensed. One of the earphones was removed and she heard Jacob whisper, "Trust us. Listen to my music. Focus on what you're feeling. Imagine we are alone. You. Me. Josh. Nothing else exists but us."

"Yes, Master."

When the earbud went back in place, her temperature rose and so did her anticipation.

Boom. Boom. Boom.

The tribal beat swirled inside her head, and the beats of her heart began to match the music.

Boom. Boom. Boom.

The earbud came out. "Don't forget your safe word, sweetheart," Josh said. "What state are you in?"

He and Jacob were taking such good care of her. They wanted to show her off, to push her boundaries. But even more they were making sure she felt safe. "Flight. I want to fly, Master."

"Very good, sub."

The earbud went back in place again.

She realized how far she'd come with them. No way would she have even considered acting this way before. No more running. The more they gave her, the more she wanted to submit to them. Her love for them continued to expand and deepen.

She felt their hands on her ass, caressing her, showing her off for their audience.

Then the first slap of one of the paddles landed in the center of her ass. It stung deliciously, but she reminded herself that they were not alone. *There are people watching. Oh God.*

Gentle caresses from her Masters eased her mind back into a state of acceptance, of submission, of trust.

Another slap. This one harder than the one before. Tears tickled her eyes. The drums rhythmic pulse continued. Another slap of the paddle and she slipped into that warm, floaty space.

Boom. Boom. Boom.

Resistance was gone. She was Josh and Jacob's prize to do with as they pleased.

Her body was warming with every slap and caress.

They removed the cuffs and rubbed her wrists. When they lifted her off the desk, they kept the blindfold and earbuds in place. One of her Masters lifted her up into his arms. She melted into Jacob, recognizing his scent with its hint of oak.

Josh kissed her. Even blindfolded, she knew his lips intimately.

They were moving her. To where? She didn't know. Another stage? She was no longer concerned with their audience. She was filled with pride that Josh and Jacob had shown her off. She felt sexy, naughty, and so turned on. *Who knew I was such an exhibitionist?* Josh and Jacob must have sensed it or else they wouldn't have set up the public scene for her.

Heat rolled through her like wild fire. They removed the earbuds. She focused, trying to make out any sounds. But she heard only the hum of what sounded to her like air conditioning. When they removed the blindfold, she knew why the sounds of the crowd at Phase Four were gone. They had taken her from the stage to a private room. They were alone.

Jacob lowered her to her feet and bent down, pressing his mouth to her lips. "You did great, angel. We're so proud of you."

"Yes, we are, sweetheart," Josh said. "Very proud."

Hearing their praise made her tingle all over.

Jacob folded a towel and placed it on the floor in front of her. "On your knees, sub."

"Yes, Master."

"Take a look around this room Master Josh and I chose for you while we prepare." Jacob slung his satchel on the table next to Josh's.

She'd been unaware of anything while they'd been on stage except the slaps to her ass and their wonderful aromas. Now, she was allowed all her senses.

She scanned the room. It had deep red walls. There was a bench and a table in the center of the space. Against the wall was a bed. Seeing Josh and Jacob put fresh sheets on the bed flooded her with excitement.

Josh and Jacob walked back to her. They stripped her out of her naughty schoolgirl outfit. They caressed her entire body without reservation. *I'm theirs and they are mine.* She felt wild and sexy.

Jacob got an electric wand from his satchel and pressed it to her nipples, delivering wonderful shocks. Josh licked her pussy, which was getting wetter and wetter.

Once again, Jacob covered her eyes with the blindfold and placed the buds in her ears. The room vanished and the tribal drums returned. More shocks and more licks. Electricity rolled through her, creating lines of energy from her throbbing nipples to her aching clit.

They guided her back on her feet and to the bench she'd seen. After they bent her over, lubricant was applied to her ass.

An earbud was removed.

"What state are you in, angel?" Jacob asked as Josh continued fingering her anus.

"Flight, Master."

He kissed her on the cheek and returned the earbud to its place. She was blazing inside and the pressure they were stoking continued to grow. She wanted them, wanted them with every ounce of her being. But they were in charge. They set the pace. She was along for the ride, a ride of pleasure that would satisfy her utterly. She felt treasured, beautiful, vulnerable— and totally safe.

Then she felt something cold on her nipples. She realized the wand was gone and that Jacob was touching her taut buds with ice. The sting drove her wild and increased her desires even more.

Josh slipped a butt plug into her ass. The stretching was intense, but once it was fully seated inside her all that remained was more need, more hunger, more want to please her Masters.

Then she felt something warm on her abdomen. The bud was removed. "What do you think this is I'm touching you with, little sub?"

"I don't know. Something metallic that's been heated a little."

"Very good. It's a spoon that I warmed up in my hands. But now I want you to stop trying to deduce what I'm touching you with and focus on how your body is responding."

"Yes, Master."

He put the earbud back in place and the drums came back.

Boom. Boom. Boom.

Jacob ran something soft over her arms, legs, and breast. As he'd commanded, she didn't try to figure out what it was. She only focused on the sensations his caresses were awakening on her tingling skin.

Josh's fingers threaded through her pussy's folds and pressed on her throbbing clit, increasing her pressure to overwhelming.

They removed the plug, the earbuds, and blindfold and lifted her off the bench. Josh carried her to the bed and stood her up next to it.

He and Jacob had stripped out of their clothes while she'd been blindfolded. Seeing their glistening muscles and hard cocks drove her mad with desire. They wanted her, and God knew she had to have them.

"Masters. Please. Please. I need you."

"And you will have us," Josh said, climbing to the bed with his back to the mattress.

Jacob lifted her off the floor. She wrapped her arms around his neck and her legs around his waist. He moved onto the mattress, lowering her down onto Josh. When she felt Josh's hands part her ass cheeks and the head of his dick press on her anus, she took in a deep breath and let it out slowly.

"That's right, angel," Jacob said. "Relax."

The plug had stretched her ass some but Josh's cock stretched her out even more.

"God, her ass feels so good." Josh's lusty tone made her tremble.

Jacob kissed her, making her toes curl. He climbed on top of her. "And I want to feel her pussy."

It felt good to be between them, to feel their bodies pressing on her skin.

The head of Jacob's cock pressed on her pussy's wet flesh. He slid his cock slowly into her body. Her Masters were inside her, both of them.

Josh began thrusting into her ass, in and out. Jacob joined in, matching his rhythm with Josh's. Even without the earbuds, she could hear the steady beat of the drums, she could feel it in her pulse. In and out. Faster and faster. Deeper and deeper. She writhed between them, clawing at their male flesh.

No more running as long as they held her. This was where she belonged. She was theirs. Forever. She would give them anything they asked. The plunges increased, pushing her past the edge.

As the explosive orgasm shot through her body, she felt them come inside her.

"Yes. Yes. God, Yes."

Chapter Twenty-Three

Several days after Destiny's Annual Paintball Extravaganza had ended, Carrie got out of the truck and looked up at the giant dragon statue in front of the O'Leary mansion.

"Sam's brother must really love dragons," she said to Josh and Jacob.

"Wait until Dragon Week next March, angel," Jacob said. "You'll learn exactly how much Patrick loves dragons."

He and Josh guided her around all the cars parked in the circular driveway. Ethel, Sam, and Patrick were throwing this party to thank all the local volunteers for the event. They were wonderful people.

Josh knocked on the door.

Sam opened it. "Welcome. It's so good to see you." He leaned over and gave her a hug.

"It's good to see you, too," she said, kissing him on the cheek.

Sam shook Josh and Jacob's hands. "Everything is ready."

They walked into the grand foyer. In the center of the space was a wooded table with Ethel's trophy lit from above.

Carrie grinned. *She deserves to be champion.*

Sam led them down a hall to the ballroom, where the party was being held. Oddly, she didn't hear any noise coming from the room. They couldn't be the first to arrive. There had been so many cars outside. *Why so quiet?*

Sam opened the large wooden doors.

She saw the crowd and heard them scream, "Welcome to Destiny, Carrie Dixon!"

"Oh my God," she said, unable to stop grinning. "How did you pull this off?"

"It's easy when Ethel is in charge," Josh said, squeezing her hand.

Jena ran up to her with Kimmie, Happiness running around their feet.

"Did we surprise you, Aunt Carrie?"

She bent down. "You sure did. I had no idea."

"Yay." Kimmie clapped her hands together. "They even made you a cake."

"They did?"

"Uh-huh."

Jena smiled. "There's more than cake in store for you, Carrie. Guys, you ready to take her to the staircase?"

"We sure are," Jacob said.

Everyone they passed on the way to the stairs welcomed her with smiles and handshakes.

"I feel like a celebrity," she whispered to Josh and Jacob.

"You are, angel," Jacob said.

At the foot of the stairs Ethel stood between Sam and Patrick. Those three looked like royalty to Carrie. The two kings with their queen.

When they reached the landing in the middle of the winding staircase, Josh and Jacob stopped.

"What are we doing, guys?" She looked out on all the wonderful people of Destiny. All eyes were on her, Josh, and Jacob. "We're holding up the party."

Josh and Jacob got down on their knees in front of her. In unison they said, "Carrie Dixon, will you make us the happiest men in the world and marry us?" Josh held her hand and Jacob brought out a big diamond engagement ring.

Stunned, she brought her hand up to her mouth. "Oh my goodness. Yes. Yes. Yes. I will marry you."

The crowd cheered, as Jacob slipped the ring on her finger. He and Josh wrapped their arms around her, drowning her in kisses.

I finally found home.

THE END

WWW.CHLOELANG.COM

ABOUT THE AUTHOR

Chloe Lang began devouring romance novels during summers between college semesters as a respite to the rigors of her studies. Soon, her lifelong addiction was born, and to this day, she typically reads three or four books every week.

For years, the very shy Chloe tried her hand at writing romance stories, but shared them with no one. After many months of prodding by an author friend, Sophie Oak, she finally relented and let Sophie read one. As the prodding turned to gentle shoves, Chloe ultimately did submit something to Siren-BookStrand. The thrill of a life happened for her when she got the word that her book would be published.

For all titles by Chloe Lang, please visit
www.bookstrand.com/chloe-lang

Siren Publishing, Inc.
www.SirenPublishing.com

Lightning Source UK Ltd.
Milton Keynes UK
UKOW06f1908010415

248975UK00018B/430/P